It wasn't anger she saw on his handsome face, but male interest—basic, primitive, potent.

"I can think of worse reasons for a guy to become the talk of the town than for people to assume he's sleeping with his pretty new waitress."

Pretty?

Roz didn't hear that word often in reference to herself. She decided that was why her chest felt tight, why her pulse had begun to pound.

And she blamed it for what happened next.

Rising to her toes she stood nearly eye-to-eye with Mason. Roz had been kissed before—by Mason, in fact, not twenty-four hours earlier. But *she* had never kissed anyone.

His eyes were as dark and delicious-looking as Hershey's syrup, and she watched them widen fractionally as he figured out her intent. Mason's eyes were definitely a window to something. His soul? Perhaps, and if that were the case, she decided his soul was beautiful. Somehow, he saw a softer, more refined version of the survivor she'd become.

He seemed to see Roz as she *wanted* to be....

Just like having a heart to heart
with your best friend, these stories will
take you from laughter to tears and back again!

Curl up and have a

HEART TO HEART

with Harlequin Romance®

So heartwarming and emotional
you'll want to have some tissues handy!

Look out for more stories in

Coming soon in Harlequin Romance:

A Family for Keeps
by Lucy Gordon, on sale May 2005

IN THE SHELTER OF HIS ARMS

Jackie Braun

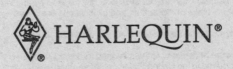

Heart *to* Heart

⬧ HARLEQUIN®

TORONTO • NEW YORK • LONDON
AMSTERDAM • PARIS • SYDNEY • HAMBURG
STOCKHOLM • ATHENS • TOKYO • MILAN • MADRID
PRAGUE • WARSAW • BUDAPEST • AUCKLAND

For Daniel,
who makes me remember what's really important!

ISBN 0-373-18186-8

IN THE SHELTER OF HIS ARMS

First North American Publication 2005.

www.eHarlequin.com

Printed in U.S.A.

CHAPTER ONE

WITH one last wheezing gasp, Old Bess died. Her demise, untimely as it was, came as no surprise to her traveling companion. The old gal was well past her prime, in deteriorating condition and had been belching black exhaust for the past dozen miles. Roz Bennett eased the ancient rusted four-door onto the side of the highway and eulogized it with a string of curses.

Climbing out to survey her surroundings, she cursed anew. Cedar trees and other evergreens towered shoulder to shoulder on each side of the two-lane road. She saw no houses, no businesses, not even a sign. She was in the middle of nowhere, on a road that seemed to be traveled by no one, and she didn't have a dime to her name.

A bitter wind smacked her face and she tucked her numb hands into the pockets of her thin jean jacket.

My luck never changes, she thought.

The sun was melting into a golden puddle in the western sky, pulling the already freezing temperature down along with it. She glanced at her wrist before remembering that she'd hocked her watch and her only pair of earrings two towns back to buy gasoline. At least half an earring's worth of fuel remained in the car's tank, for all the good it would do her now.

Grabbing her duffel bag out of the car's back seat, she debated her options.

A few miles earlier, she'd passed a roadside bar. If they had a pool table, she could hustle herself a meal and maybe make enough cash for a cheap motel room someplace. But forward was the only direction Roz believed in traveling. Decision made, she began walking.

Less than a mile later, she was wondering just how long it took to freeze to death when she heard the Jeep. Actually she thought it might have been the loud thump of bass that first snagged her attention rather than the shiny red sport utility vehicle's finely tuned engine. Walking backward, she stuck out her thumb, but needn't have bothered. The driver was already slowing, easing the SUV onto the shoulder just behind her.

It was a man.

Roz hunched her shoulders and pretended to be unconcerned that she was a lone female walking down the side of a deserted highway at dusk.

The man rolled down the window as he flipped off the music. "Hello."

"Hey."

Now that she had a good look at him, she guessed him to be in his mid-thirties. His hair was straight and the color of strong coffee. He wore it short and tidy. His eyes were dark and she got the feeling his steady gaze didn't miss much. Still, the lines that fanned out toward his temples looked like the kind put there by laughter and time spent outdoors rather than squinty-eyed meanness. Overall, he looked reputable enough. She felt her muscles uncoil slightly.

"That your car back there?" He hitched a thumb over his shoulder and motioned.

Roz nodded, deciding to keep her answers brief and noncommittal. "Engine trouble."

He made what might have been a sympathetic noise in the back of his throat before asking, ''Where you heading?''

West, she almost said. It would have been the truth, but since most people expected a destination rather than a direction, she figured it would make him suspicious. And the last thing Roz wanted to do was make the one person who stood between her and frostbite uncomfortable. So she said, ''Wisconsin.'' It was the next state she would come to on her journey west, so it wasn't exactly a lie.

''Afraid I'm not going that far.''

''Oh.'' Her feet felt frozen to the ground. ''Where are you going?''

''Chance Harbor. It's northwest of here, on Superior's shore, about halfway between the Porcupine Mountains and Hancock. I can drop you in one of the little towns we come to before we hit North U.S. 45,'' he offered. ''There's bound to be a repair shop.''

''Chance Harbor,'' she repeated. ''I don't recall seeing it on the map.''

He grunted out a laugh. ''It's so small it doesn't make many maps, but ask any fisherman and he'll know the place. Some call it Last Chance Harbor, because it's one of the few safe places to ride out a storm before heading up around the Keweenaw Peninsula.''

A safe place, she thought. Was there really such a thing? In twenty-six years, she had yet to find one. Still, she liked the name. And, since her entire life had been one big messy work of fate, not helped in the least by her impulsive nature, she made up her mind.

''I'll go there.''

''To Chance Harbor?'' Dark eyebrows shot up in surprise and she wasn't blind to the speculation she saw brewing in his gaze. ''What about your car?''

''It's not going anywhere,'' she said flatly. ''I'm surprised it made it the past few hundred miles.''

''Chance Harbor is a little out of the way if you'll be heading to Wisconsin.''

''That's okay, I'll consider it the scenic route. I need to gct a temporary job anyway. Think I might find work there? I'm running a little low on spending money.''

Low, as in none, she thought grimly.

''It's off season for tourists, but there might be something, nothing that will pay more than minimum wage, mind you.''

Roz was already tossing her duffel bag into the vehicle's back seat when she said, "That's good enough for me."

When they were back on the road, he turned up the music again, but not nearly as loud. Still, it hammered through the Jeep and seemed to echo through the empty cavern of her stomach. When exactly had she last eaten? Could the five lint-covered M&Ms she'd found in her jacket pocket that morning be considered a meal? She decided to concentrate on the music instead.

Roz never would have taken the man for an AC/DC fan. Top Forty, maybe. And, based on the down jacket and faded denim he wore and the fact that they were out in the sticks, country music. Put him in a cowboy hat and spurs and lash him to the back of a bucking bronco, and he'd look right at home. But he seemed too clean-cut, too George Strait-ish to enjoy the raunchy lyrics and gyrating rhythms of hard rock. Yet, she could see his thumbs tapping discreetly on the steering wheel in time to the bass and she got the feeling if she weren't in the truck he'd be belting out the words to the very appropriate "Highway to Hell."

He glanced her way. "I'm Mason, by the way. Mason Striker."

"Roz."

He waited a beat, apparently for a last name. When she didn't oblige, he thankfully didn't press. "Nice to meet you, Roz. Let me know if you get too warm."

Too warm? She nearly laughed. She'd lost all feeling in her toes and was at the point that taking a blowtorch to them would have been welcome. But she said, "I'll do that."

She settled back in her seat, stretching out her legs. The hot air that blasted out of the vents began to thaw her extremities. Her car had stopped giving out anything but lukewarm air more than a week ago, so heat was a forgotten luxury. And lately, sleep was as well. She leaned her head back against the padded rest, intending only to relax. She was unaware she'd closed her eyes and drifted off until someone began to shake her arm.

The woman came awake quickly, much the way a rattlesnake would if someone disturbed its nest, Mason thought. Fight or flight. He could all but see the adrenaline shoot through her bloodstream, making either a possibility.

"What?" she asked defensively, hands balling into pathetically small fists. Still, he didn't doubt she would use them if provoked. He decided to pretend not to notice her edgy reaction.

In his previous line of work, he'd seen that type of response before. The reasons behind it were never good. In fact, they usually made the six o'clock news, which was partly why Mason had moved back to Chance Harbor. He no longer wanted to try to solve other people's problems, which at the moment seemed a bit hypocritical since he'd given the woman a ride. But he couldn't very well have left her on the side of the highway in subzero temperatures. A ride would be the end of it, he assured himself. And yet, as he switched off the ignition and climbed out, he heard himself say, "Come on inside. We'll see if we can find you a place to stay."

Roz got out of the vehicle slowly, hesitant to leave its warmth, which was fading already. The sun had all but set, making it hard to see anything but the building in front of them.

"Where are we?"

"The Lighthouse Tavern."

"I can read," she said, trying not to seem defensive, even though she hadn't quite managed to sound through the letters on the flashing neon sign. "Why are we stopping here?"

"End of the trail," he said. "You can make arrangements for your car, and telephone around for a place to stay."

Roz couldn't afford a cardboard box at this point, but he didn't give her a chance to say so. He walked through the front entrance to a chorus of cowbells, giving her little choice but to follow.

The interior of the Lighthouse Tavern hadn't changed much in the years since Mason's grandfather, Daniel Striker, had built it. Mason always felt as if he was coming home when he walked inside. Since it had passed from his father's hands to his own a year earlier, he'd done some updating, just as his father had done before him. The tables and chairs were new, and so were the jukebox, big-screen television and pool table. But the wide bar that swept across the back of the room was the original mahogany, as was the brass kicker rail that ran just below it.

Of course, he'd never intended to be a bar owner. He'd wanted something far more adventurous than that. And he'd gotten it.

In spades.

He rubbed his shoulder and felt the ache from the old wound. A bullet could do a lot of damage to a body, and even more to the psyche, a shrink had told him. As if it took a master's degree in psychology to figure that out. He shrugged off the intrusive memory. He'd come back to forget, not to dwell on all that had gone wrong.

The crowd in the Lighthouse Tavern was light, but it was early yet. Unlike his father and grandfather, Mason didn't worry much about the bottom line. He ran the tavern more for something to do than to make a living. He had enough money in the bank so that if he were frugal, he'd never have to work again. He rubbed his shoulder. His flush bank account had not come cheaply.

He watched the young woman look around the tavern. He'd lay odds her twitchy gaze had already located the exits. But all she said was, "Cool place."

"I like it. Have a seat."

She eased onto one of the high stools and was not quick enough to hide her surprise when he flipped up a hinged section of mahogany just to her right and walked behind the bar.

"You work here?"

"Something like that. I own the place."

"You don't look like a bar owner."

"What do bar owners look like?" he asked, vaguely amused.

She shrugged. "I don't know. Bad teeth, greasy hair, big guts, tattoos."

"No to the first three."

"You have a tattoo?"

He merely smiled. "Can I get you anything?"

Mason thought he heard her stomach rumble, as if in anticipation, but she shook her head. "Nah, I'm fine."

"You sure? It's on the house," he prodded.

He swore she almost sagged with relief.

"Well, a cola then."

When he turned back from getting a clean glass, he caught her helping herself to a fistful of beer nuts from a bowl near her elbow. He set the beverage in front of her, nudged the beer nuts closer and handed her a portable phone.

"Casey's Garage is probably your best bet."

Before he could look up the telephone number, she was resting a hand on the back of his and shaking her head. "Look, the best mechanic in the world isn't going to save that car. And even if it could be saved, I can't afford to have it towed here. Do you know anybody who would just take it for scrap?"

He glanced briefly at the hand she had yet to remove. The fine-boned hand whose fingers felt like icicles and yet left his skin feeling oddly singed. He chalked it up to a year's worth of abstinence.

"Sure." He pivoted away, breaking contact, and hollered down the bar. "Hey, Mickey. They still taking scrap at that yard near Bruce Crossing?"

"Last I heard."

"You interested in towing this lady's car there?"

"Sure."

"I can't pay him," she whispered.

Looking at her, Mason added, "She'll

give you whatever the car gets, unless it's more than a hundred bucks.''

Mickey shrugged. ''Okay, where's the car?''

''About five miles east of Forty-Five on the shoulder of M-28.''

Mickey nodded once and rubbed his chin. ''Probably the only one there, but just in case, what color is it?''

''Rust,'' Mason replied, deadpan.

Roz laughed, hesitantly at first and then louder. And he would have bet the bar that it was the first genuine laugh she'd enjoyed in a very long time. Again, he found himself wondering what her story was. What made her so guarded, so edgy? And, again, he promised himself he was not going to get involved.

It was full dark outside and Roz supposed she should be leaving, but she didn't have anyplace to go and she had just, finally, gotten warm. Mason had headed off behind the swinging doors she assumed led to the kitchen, but it didn't bother her to be sitting alone as the crowd thickened. A couple of guys were playing pool now and she thought about getting in on a game. They knew how to play, but she figured she was better. A meal often had depended on her well-honed skill with a cue stick.

She'd eaten enough beer nuts to take the bite off her hunger, but she wouldn't mind something more substantial. She was about to saunter over and introduce herself when Mason returned.

"Hey, Roz, you need a job, right?"

She straightened in her seat. "Yeah."

"You ever waitress before?"

"A time or two."

"Well, one of my waitresses just quit and the other is home with the flu. If you're interested, you'll have to start right now. Work's not bad and the tips are pretty decent."

Roz struggled to keep her grin in check. "Well, I guess I can help you out."

An hour later, she was pulling a draft from the tap with one hand and adding a fruit garnish to a vodka sour with the other.

"I guess you weren't lying when you said you'd done this before," Mason said from behind her.

He was close, but not inappropriately close, despite the tight quarters behind the bar. Even so, she was sure he would touch her, even just on the pretext of brushing past her. But he merely set a couple of burgers down on a tray atop the bar and moved a little farther away.

"Yeah. I've also worked as a cashier, sold feed at a grainery, been a short order cook, a janitor and, most recently, a blackjack dealer at the casino in St. Ignace."

"Any other talents?" There was no double entendre in the way he said it. No leer in the open, interested way in which he regarded her.

"I'm a well of untapped potential."

She sobered after she said it. That's what her caseworker had told her…right after Roz had been shuttled to yet another foster home.

Mason didn't seem to notice her sudden mood change.

"Good to know," he said, and winked. Then he tilted his head, all business again. "See that guy at the end of the bar?"

"Yeah."

"That's Big Bob Bailey. He's been coming to the Lighthouse since my granddad owned the place. Fix him a whiskey, neat, when you get a chance."

And then he walked away.

The night was winding down. Only a few men remained hunched over their drinks at the bar. Mason had put the chairs on top of the tables and was sweeping up a small mountain of popcorn and beer nuts. In the kitchen, the cook was preparing the next day's soup. He was an older man named Bergen. Whether that was his first name or last, Roz wasn't sure. But she did know it was *his* kitchen. Or so he'd informed her the one time she'd poked her head through the swinging doors and tried to steal a French fry.

Roz was bone-tired and hungry enough that the beer nuts, which had gone down like prime rib a few hours ago, were looking like fine cuisine again. But she had thirty-two dollars in tips weighing down her pockets and, better than that, she'd solved the mystery of where she would be sleeping that night. As she washed the last of the heavy glass mugs, Mason walked over.

"I've got some paperwork for you to fill out."

"Sure."

She came around the bar and sat on the same high stool she'd first occupied. The tavern looked different now that the lights were on. She glanced at some of the pictures that hung framed on the wall next to a wide shelf of liquor bottles. Family pictures, or so they seemed. Black and white or color, they showed men and women of varying ages, holding hands, hugging, laughing. Children in their Sunday best posed for the camera, smiling widely. The photographs made the bar seem almost homey. The envy came quickly, and even now it surprised her. How many years had she chased the dream of having her own family?

"Here's an application and W-4 so Uncle Sam can take his cut." He handed her a ballpoint. "Want a beer or something?"

"Sure. Beer's fine."

The application was standard and easy to read, which Roz appreciated since she'd never earned her high school diploma. Even before calling it quits, reading had been difficult for her. If not for the school district's policy of social promotion, she figured she would have wound up the oldest elementary student in Metro Detroit. As it was, she had been two grades back by the time she'd turned eighteen. With the state no longer acting as her guardian, she'd been free to drop out. Functionally illiterate is what one of her guidance counselors had called her particular limitation. Roz knew some people thought she was just stupid.

Mason ushered the stragglers out the door after being assured that the sober one among them would be driving the other two home. When he turned, he caught sight of the woman he'd hired so spontaneously earlier that evening. He still wasn't sure exactly why he'd done it. After he'd been shot, hadn't he sworn off helping out damsels in distress and other assorted strays?

Of course, he did need another hand in the bar, and it wasn't as if he had a stack of applications to choose from. That was the only reason he'd reached out to this prickly, seemingly desperate woman, he assured himself.

He studied her profile as she filled out the form he'd given her. Her head was angled studiously, tongue caught between slightly crooked front teeth. He didn't want to admit that something about her tugged at him.

Attraction? He did find her pretty, almost in spite of her features. Her hair was dirty blond and boy short. It stuck up at the crown and did a little U-turn around a cowlick above her left temple. He'd lay odds that she'd cut it herself. Her eyes were a smoky-blue, their heavy lids devoid of cosmetics, as were her lips, which were by far her most feminine feature. She was tall, just half a head shorter than he, and wand thin, the kind of thin that came not from diet and exercise but nerves and not enough to eat. Give her a month of decent meals, and he decided she'd have a first-class figure. Those long legs already made a man's mouth water. He curbed the thought and walked over to where she sat.

"Almost done," she said, sounding defensive.

"No hurry." He read over her shoulder, but if he'd hoped to satisfy his curiosity, he was mistaken. Half of the form was blank, the other half filled out in the kind of careful block letters a child might use.

She listed no street address or telephone number, no next of kin and no date of birth, but her full name caught his attention: Rosalind Bennett. The name seemed too soft for the hard-edged woman who gripped the pen with fingers that had calluses and nails bitten to the quick. And yet Roz didn't quite fit, either. She finished writing and handed him the application, gaze defiant, almost as if daring him to complain.

"I don't mind the blanks, but I do need a date of birth."

She blinked, and he knew she'd been prepared for some kind of confrontation. "I'm twenty-six as of February first."

"That's today...yesterday," he said, glancing at the clock. She showed no emotion, not even a flicker of a smile when he added, "Happy birthday."

"What time do you need me here tomorrow?" She walked to the end of the bar where she'd stowed her duffel bag and jean jacket earlier.

"Six, a little early if you want to eat before your shift. A free meal is one of the perks of employment. You get one half-hour break around nine, but most people like to eat earlier."

Roz shrugged into her coat and swung the bag over her shoulder. "See you tomorrow."

She was almost to the door when Mason remembered his manners. "Hey, wait. I don't know what I was thinking. You don't have a place to stay."

"I've got a place, don't worry."

"Oh." He frowned. "Then let me give you a ride. You don't have a car."

"No need for a ride."

She slipped out the door and was gone before he could grab his coat. He wondered where she would be sleeping and how she had found a place to stay when she'd been working all night. Then he recalled a couple of snowmobilers who'd kind of hit on her a few hours before closing. They weren't regulars, probably downstaters who'd come north to travel the area's abundance of groomed trails. They were probably at the motel half a mile down the road.

Well, Roz Bennett wasn't his concern. As long as she showed up for work tomorrow, he didn't care where she slept. Or, he tried to convince himself, with whom.

Roz walked around to the back of the bar and ducked behind the Dumpster. She hoped it wouldn't take Mason and Bergen long to finish up and leave. But it was a good fifteen minutes before she heard the bar door creak open. A light snow was falling and her feet were already turning to ice blocks inside her sneakers.

"About time," she muttered, when she heard Mason call good night to the cook. Vehicle doors slammed shut. One engine fired to life, followed by another. Then gravel crunched, gears shifted and the men were gone.

She took her hands out of her pockets, rubbed them together for warmth and then set to work stacking wooden palettes. When she had half a dozen of them in a pile, she hoisted herself on top, stood and tugged at the small rest room window that she'd unlocked earlier in the evening. It stuck at first, making her wonder if maybe it had been painted shut. But then it gave way with a noisy squawk. Her conscience only bothered her a little when she followed her duffel bag through the opening and dropped down inside.

Morning came before Roz was ready for it, but then she was used to running on only a few hours of sleep. She'd bunked on the floor of a small storeroom off the kitchen, using her duffel bag as a pillow. Now, with sunlight slinking through the window, she realized the room also doubled as Mason's office. A large wooden desk dominated one corner of the room. It was old, but well cared for and neatly polished. The computer and fax machine on its surface appeared to be new and top of the line. Standing sentinel next to the desk was a four-drawer metal filing cabinet, atop which sat the sorriest-looking plant Roz had ever seen.

"Real green thumb," she murmured as she stood and stretched.

Shelves along the wall by the door held inventory, everything from pickles for the burgers to margarita mix and extra beer nuts. Her stomach growled, reminding her that it hadn't forgotten it was empty. She pushed hunger from her mind and thumbed through a pile of paperbacks stacked on a shelf that ran just below the window. They were thick books, filled with big words. Some of them she recognized, the rest she would have to carefully sound out and even then she wasn't sure she would know their meaning. Again, she felt the sharp stab of disappointment that she couldn't read well enough to enjoy it. It seemed to her the cheapest form of escape on the planet. From the well-worn pages of the paperbacks, she decided Mason thought so, too.

She wandered to the kitchen, bravely pushing through the door because she knew the cook wouldn't be there. She'd just help herself to a little something, maybe toast or juice, anything to give her the energy to leave the warm confines of the tavern and walk in the frigid temperatures till she found a restaurant serving breakfast. She found a loaf of bread on one of the shelves by the stove and filched two slices. Rummaging around the huge stainless-steel refrigerator, she came up with some butter. That's all she intended to take, but the ham caught her eye and her mouth watered. Protein, and not in the form of a beer nut. She nearly wept.

She was cutting off a thick slab of the smoked meat when she heard the locks on the front door begin to rattle. Roz didn't wait around to wonder who it was. She stuffed the rest of the ham back in the fridge, tucked the bread and slice of meat she'd hacked off down the front of her shirt and hightailed it to the rest room. Through a crack, she watched Mason walk in, a pretty woman close behind him. The momentary twinge of disappointment caught Roz off-guard. So, he was taken. Big deal. She should have guessed it. Men that good-looking and kind were never single.

Quietly she closed the door and climbed atop the heat register. She was out the window and standing on the wooden palettes before she remembered her duffel bag was still in Mason's office.

CHAPTER TWO

MASON loved his sister Marnie dearly, but she could be a trial, and that was putting it politely. She was five years his junior, and yet since their parents had retired to Arizona, she mothered him mercilessly. She was also recently married, which meant she was determined that everyone who was not married or headed to the altar needed to be helped in that direction. She'd made it her mission in life.

"I'm just saying that you've been back in Chance Harbor for a year and you haven't dated anyone."

He set the toolbox he was carrying on the bar and shrugged out of his down jacket. "And you know this how exactly?"

Marnie rolled her eyes. She was as tall as his six feet in her heeled boots, and she took advantage of this fact by rising on tiptoe and looking down her nose at him.

"It doesn't take great detective work to

figure it out, Mase. You're moody, you work every night and weekend, and Penny at the Shop-and-Save says you buy microwave dinners in bulk.''

"God love a small town,'' he muttered. "Any other rumors floating around about me?''

"Not a rumor, exactly.''

He angled his head to the side, and even though he knew he would regret asking, he said, "What?''

"Just that term limits mean Representative Westin won't be running again for the state Legislature. A lot of folks around here think you'd be a good choice.''

"Marnie, no. I'm not cut out for politics.''

"You're too honest, I know, but I think that would be your appeal, Mason. Your talents are being wasted here.''

That stopped him in his tracks. "I like tending bar.''

"As a hobby, maybe. But this isn't your life.''

"It was good enough for Dad and Granddad.''

"That was their choice. The Lighthouse

Tavern was their dream. For you, it's just a convenient place to hide."

"I'm not hiding. I'm recuperating."

"Mason..."

"End of discussion."

He was heading to his office when he heard the front door jangle open.

"Good morning," a voice called.

He turned to find his new waitress standing just inside the door. The early-morning sunlight behind her cast her in silhouette, and yet even if she had not spoken, even if she had remained obscured in shadow, Mason would have known her. Too thin, he thought again.

"Good morning," he called.

She took a couple of hesitant steps forward, far enough inside to bring her features into focus. As he watched, she smiled anxiously and divided a careful look between him and Marnie. His stomach did an odd little roll when he noticed she was wearing the same thing she'd had on the previous day. Before he could stop himself, he wondered again where she'd passed the night...and with whom. She didn't seem the easy sort, but he doubted the money she'd earned in tips the night before had been enough to buy a room at the motel.

"Hey, I did say six o'clock, didn't I?"

"Yeah." For the first time since he'd met her, she appeared truly nervous. "I...I was out for a walk and saw you come in. I thought maybe you could use a hand early."

"I'm just here to see about the sink in the men's room. It's been draining a little slow lately." He consulted his watch. "Your shift doesn't start for nine hours."

"I know." She licked her lips and he got the feeling she was searching for another excuse, and he'd be damned if he could figure out why.

Marnie nudged his ribs. "Aren't you going to introduce us?"

"Oh, sure. Marnie, this is Rose, the waitress I hired to replace Carol. Marnie is my sister."

"It's Roz," she replied at the same time Marnie said, "Carol quit?"

"Yesterday. Bob decided to head downstate to look for work." For Roz's benefit, he added, "Bob's her husband, and he's been out of work since last winter."

"What are you doing in Chance

Harbor?'' Marnie asked, appalling Mason with her lack of manners. But the woman didn't seem bothered by the question.

"Looking for work.''

Marnie laughed outright. "Not many people come to the Upper Peninsula to look for work, honey. You sure you didn't mean to head south instead?''

"Rose is actually heading west. She's going to Wisconsin,'' Mason added.

"Roz,'' she corrected again. "My ride died. Mason stopped and picked me up. I'll just be in Chance Harbor until I make enough to buy another used car and then I'll be on my way.''

Marnie's gaze shifted to Mason. "I thought you were through playing Good Samaritan, brother?''

"Drop it, Marnie.''

She smiled knowingly. "You can't change who you are. Not even politics could change who you are. That's why people want you to run for office. They're tired of campaign promises that never material-ize. They want someone they can trust to do what's right.''

"Rose isn't interested in your penny psychology,'' he said. "Why don't you do something useful, like make a pot of coffee?''

His sister stuck out her tongue at him, but she slipped behind the bar and went to work. As she measured coffee grounds into a filter, she said, ''So, where are you staying?''

Again, Rose looked nervous. ''No place I care to stay for long.''

''Let me guess,'' Marnie replied. ''The old place out by the grainery. The Bates Motel is more inviting.''

Rose said nothing, but Mason cleared his throat.

''You know, it occurred to me last night that I should have given you an advance on your salary.'' When Rose just stared at him, he continued, ''You know, for living expenses.''

''I'll get by okay till payday,'' she said stiffly.

Pride, he decided. Standing there in her faded jeans and her thin denim jacket, she had it in abundance.

''Just the same, I'd feel better knowing you had a little extra.'' Mind made up, he said, ''Come on back to the office.''

She did as he asked, looking all the

while as if he were leading her to the gallows. When Mason opened the door, he thought he understood why. He noticed the duffel bag right away. He practically had to step over it to walk to his desk. But he pretended not to see. He needed to think.

The significance of the bag was obvious. She'd been inside his bar after closing, doing God only knew what. Was she some sort of rip-off artist? He dismissed the thought immediately. She looked too thin and desperate to be any good at running a con. Still, it hit him exactly how little he knew about the woman named Rosalind Bennett. The woman he'd picked up on the highway because she'd been by herself and even here in the sticks, things could happen to a lone female. Good Samaritan, Marnie had called him. But he shrugged off the title. He didn't want it any longer. It had only brought him grief.

For all he knew, she could be a drug addict or a common thief.

Last night's take was locked in the top drawer of his desk. Did she know that? The desk didn't look disturbed, but had she been trying to gain access just before he and Marnie walked through the front door?

Marnie, of course, would have blasted Rose with a full arsenal of questions, right after she'd slugged her a good one in the eye. That was his sister, all passion and punch. Mason, on the other hand, preferred to think of himself as the patient sort. He'd wait, like a cat watching a mouse, until he knew for sure what game this young woman was playing. He wasn't reserving judgment, he told himself. He was merely being practical. He needed a waitress and so far she'd proven herself to be a damn good one. First sign of trouble, he'd cut her loose without so much as a prick of conscience.

When he turned from his desk with the check, she had the duffel bag looped nonchalantly over one shoulder. The bag wasn't huge, but it seemed to dwarf her slender frame, causing her to slouch forward a bit. Still, he didn't comment on it and neither did she.

"That's really not necessary," she said quietly.

He pushed the check into her hand. "It is."

He wasn't being a chump, he assured himself. It was basic human kindness. The shadowed look in her eyes made him think she hadn't experienced much recently. Besides, the sum on the check wouldn't set him back any if she took off before earning it.

She didn't look him in the eye when she mumbled her thanks. Did that proclaim her guilt or confirm her embarrassment?

"There's a bank next to the bakery in town. They'll cash it for you without an account. It's Saturday, but they're open till noon."

She nodded and fiddled with the buttons on her worn jacket. The coat had seen better days, as had the rest of what she was wearing.

"Oh, and I forgot to give you this last night." He pulled a large box off the bottom shelf from next to the pickles and opened the flaps. After pawing around inside of it for a few seconds, he came out with a couple of blue chambray shirts.

"I figure a medium will do. You're skinny, but your arms are long."

He held up one of the shirts, the breast pocket of which was emblazoned with the name of the bar. If the clothes in that duffel bag were as worn as what she had on, he figured she could use something new. When she just stood there staring at the shirts he held out, he tossed them at her.

''Consider them a uniform.''

Roz was too stupefied to do more than hold out a hand to catch the shirts he flung in her direction. The man was insane. Had to be. Or else blind, because only the visually impaired could have missed the duffel bag that had been sitting in the middle of the floor, obvious as an elephant, when they entered the small room. The bag announced her guilt clearly, irrefutably. It had breaking and entering written all over it. Yet he'd stepped around it, written her a check and was now giving her clothing.

She didn't trust him. She didn't trust anyone. And yet he seemed to trust her. Roz had long grown accustomed to suspicion. She'd been thrown out of department stores based on her appearance alone, and yet this man was advancing her money, acting as if he believed she would be back to earn it. Funny, but she hadn't wanted to run away until now.

''It's too much,'' she said hoarsely, not even looking at the amount he'd filled in on the check.

"You'll work hard."

"Hope you like your coffee black," Marnie said as she came through the door carrying two mugs. She handed one to Roz and kept the other for herself. "You can get your own, brother dear."

Oblivious to the tension, she sipped her coffee and said, "You never did say where you were staying, Rose."

"It's Roz," she said absently. "I'm staying…"

She looked at the check and the shirts lying over the crook of her elbow. Then her gaze connected with Mason's, connected with those dark eyes that seemed to peer into her soul.

"The truth is, I slept in here last night. I climbed through the bathroom window after you and Bergen left, and I slept on the floor. Thanks for letting me work last night. I made enough in tips to get me to the next town."

She handed Mason the check, then the shirts and finally the steaming mug of coffee. Hiking the duffel bag higher onto her shoulder, she turned to leave.

Mason opened his mouth to call her back, but in the end he needn't have bothered to try to stop her. She did that all on her own. Three steps into the hallway, she fainted dead away.

Roz came to slowly. Mortification charged well ahead of her weak pulse when she realized she was lying on the floor of the Lighthouse Tavern. The owner was pillowing her head with his big hands, concern etched on his handsome face.

"God," she sighed, and closed her eyes. "I can't even exit right."

"You exited just fine, right onto my floor. When was the last time you ate anything?"

She thought about the ham and twin slices of bread tucked away in her shirt, so near to her empty stomach and yet so far.

"I had something yesterday."

"Besides beer nuts?" he asked pointedly.

She didn't answer. It seemed too pitiful to mention the five linty M&Ms.

"You know, kiddo," Marnie said, peering over her brother's shoulder, "the idiot who said you can never be too rich or too thin died a slow death from starvation after the weight of her diamond rings kept her from getting to the dinner table.''

"Marnie, do something useful and get Rose something to eat, would ya?''

"It's Roz,'' she sighed, not that anyone seemed to hear her.

Mason's sister was muttering, ''Marnie do this, Marnie do that. And never a please or thank you.'' But even as she groused, she was leaving to do his bidding.

"Are you going to call the cops?'' Roz asked when they were alone.

"Last I heard fainting wasn't a criminal offense.''

"Breaking and entering is.''

He acknowledged her crime with a curt nod, and then surprised her by saying, ''But that wasn't your intent, was it. You just needed a place to sleep. I'd have given you a key, you know, or lent you the money for a motel room.''

Why, she wondered, and her confusion must have shown on her face, because he said, ''This is Chance Harbor. It's a small town. We help people out if they need it, Rose.''

She didn't correct him this time. Clearly he saw her as something other than what she was and she decided that wasn't bad for a change. She sat up slowly to keep the world from spinning out of control again. He helped, one arm around her shoulders.

"I'm sorry, Mason."

And since coming clean seemed the order of the day, she dipped inside her shirt, pulled out the ham and bread, and handed them to him. "I took this. I planned to pay you for it, really."

His voice was gruff when he said, "Just eat it, Rose."

She ate like a longshoreman. Mason had never seen a woman put away so much food in one sitting. After the ham and bread, to which Marnie had added mustard and a lettuce garnish, Rose downed a Western omelet, three fat slices of bacon, a glass of orange juice and three cups of coffee. Perched on a stool at the bar, she reminded him of a squirrel, storing nuts away in anticipation of a long, cold winter. And though she didn't say a word during the entire meal, the way her hands shook as she held the fork spoke eloquently about her past.

And, despite his many resolutions not to

get involved, Mason wanted to know more. His curiosity was that of an employer, he told himself.

When she drained the third cup of coffee, he asked, "Care to fill in some of those blanks on your application now?"

It was a question, not a command. Roz carefully wiped her mouth with the paper napkin Marnie had provided somewhere between the sandwich and the omelet. She figured she owed him—for the meal, the kindness, at the very least for not calling the police.

"What blank do you want filled in first?"

He didn't hesitate. "Is Rosalind Bennett your real name?"

"No."

His eyebrows hitched up, but he didn't respond. He merely waited for her to continue. She liked that about him, all that quiet patience. Most people badgered and bullied. And so she told him what she rarely told anyone.

"I don't know my real name."

The old shame was there in the quietly spoken words. She wondered if she would ever get past it, even as she told herself it didn't really matter. None of it *really* mattered. That, of course, had been her mantra for as long as she could remember.

"Amnesia?" Marnie asked. She rested an elbow on the bar and cupped her hand in her chin, enthralled. Roz chuckled. She liked this Marnie, even if the woman apparently watched too much daytime television.

"Nothing that…medical. I was abandoned as a toddler."

"Oh my God!" Marnie's eyes rounded to the size of small saucers. Mason's reaction was much more dispassionate, even though his features softened.

"Who gave you your name, then?"

"The state. They also gave me my birth date."

A pair of dark eyebrows pulled together in confusion. "Okay, you lost me."

"No, someone lost me on February first, twenty-three years ago. Police found me wandering around in a diaper and little else at the intersection of Rosalind Street and Bennett Avenue in Detroit. Rosalind Bennett, get it?"

"Aw, Rose," she thought she heard him murmur.

She shrugged, uncomfortable with the sympathy she saw in his eyes. "It's not a bad name. I mean, it has Jane Doe beat all to hell."

"What happened then?" Marnie wanted to know.

Roz picked up her fork and toyed with the stingy remains of her breakfast. "Foster care."

Two words that said nothing and yet, in Roz's mind, they said it all.

"What about adoption?" Mason asked softly.

Ah, yes, she thought, the happily-ever-after she'd quit believing in not long after she'd figured out the truth about the Easter Bunny.

"I almost got adopted once. First people who had me. I stayed with them until I was six. They were nice. Older couple. The man had a white beard. He reminded me of Santa Claus. They'd been doing the foster parenting thing for years. They'd adopted a dozen other kids, or something like that. Some of them still lived at home."

"What happened?"

Something changed about her then. Mason saw it immediately, the way the shutters came down, closing off any vulnerability.

"Didn't work out," she said simply, but he knew there was nothing simple about it or the heartache it must have caused.

Why? The question swirled in his mind, but Mason managed to keep from voicing it. Over Rose's head he sent Marnie a warning glance just in case her curiosity got ahead of her manners on this subject.

But Marnie asked rather generically, "What happened then?"

The young woman fiddled with her napkin, shredding it into neat little pieces of confetti. Despite the show of nervous energy, her tone was indifferent when she continued. They might have been chatting about the weather for all the emotion she showed, but her words and the images they conjured up chilled Mason to the bone.

"Let's see, I got bounced to five other homes after that. Ran away from three of them. Did six months in juvie for...a little misunderstanding."

"Was there nowhere you could turn for help?" Mason asked softly.

The tone, more than his words, made her eyes sting. She took a moment to regroup, brushing the shredded napkin into a pile on the bar as she brushed away the memories she rarely allowed close. In the end, ignoring his question seemed the best solution.

"The day I turned eighteen, the state said, we're done with you. So, I packed up my stuff and left foster home number six."

"Have you ever looked for your biological family?" Marnie asked.

"No. They didn't want me."

"How can you be so sure? I'd want to meet them, confront them, at the very least. You must have questions."

Oh, she did. A lifetime of questions, stored up and safely locked away. It wasn't the questions that bothered her as much as knowing that she might not like the answers.

"Quit badgering her, Marnie. You'll give her indigestion." Mason smiled at Roz after he said it.

She watched his lips twitch. He had a great mouth. And the mouth went nicely with the Cary Grant dent in his chin and the coal-colored eyes that seemed to peer into her soul.

He sees too much, Roz thought, not for the first time.

''Well, thanks for breakfast.'' She pushed her plate away and stood. What should she do now? Leaving seemed in order. It surprised her that she wanted to stay. From the pocket of her jeans, she pulled the check Mason had insisted on giving her a second time after she'd come to. After carefully smoothing out the creases, she set it next to her empty juice cup.

''I really appreciate everything you've done for me.'' Her voice had dropped to an embarrassing whisper.

''You're welcome.'' He stood as well. ''I'll drive you to the bank. You'll cash that and then we'll find you a place to stay. You should have a chance to get settled in before your shift tonight.''

''You want me to stay?''

He ignored her question, as did Marnie, who pointed out, ''The motel will set her back sixty bucks a night.''

''Sixty a night?'' Roz echoed, feeling queasy, whether from the big meal or the thought of spending every penny she made on lodgings when she needed to save to buy a car. ''I can't afford to drop more than four hundred bucks a week on a room.''

"I'll talk to Clara. Try to work something out."

Roz assumed this Clara must be the owner.

Marnie shook her head. "It's snowmobile season, Mase. She's not going to budge, especially when she's trying to recover from a couple of months of bad business." For Roz's benefit, she said, "Too much rain this fall and the trees dropped their leaves early."

After a couple of minutes of thinking, Marnie announced, "I've got it! How about your garage apartment?" Something about the gleam in her eyes made Roz slightly nervous.

It must have made Mason nervous, too. For the first time since she'd known him, he stumbled around for words.

"It's...it's not that big."

"Aw, come on, Mase. It's perfect." To Roz she said, "It's just a little apartment, pretty much all one room with a bath, but it's adorable."

"I can't afford much," Roz emphasized, but she might as well have been talking to herself.

"I lived there briefly before I got married last summer. I'd let you stay with us, but we're remodeling right now. We've got half the house torn up.''

Roz didn't know which sounded worse: the prospect of sharing a house with two newlyweds or living a stone's throw away from her handsome new boss.

''She can walk to work,'' Marnie said.

That cozy, albeit practical arrangement had Mason stammering again. ''It...it needs work.''

Marnie waved off his concern. ''New curtains at the window, a little elbow grease and it will be good as new.''

''Fine.'' Rising from his chair he pulled on his coat. ''Oil up your arm and get started while Rose and I are at the bank.''

CHAPTER THREE

MASON STRIKER lived in a lighthouse perched on Superior's rocky shore. A real, working lighthouse that cast its beacon out over the largest and coldest of the Great Lakes. And it was indeed walking distance from the tavern whose name it had inspired.

"I didn't know you could own a lighthouse. When was it built?" Roz asked.

"It's a bit of a relic. The cornerstone says 1852. My great-grandfather was the third caretaker back when the light was still manual. Nowadays, technology makes that kind of a job all but obsolete. The state comes in periodically to ensure the light is working. Other than that, it's pretty much like living in any other house, except for the solitude and great view."

He called it a relic, but to Roz's way of thinking, the stone foundation and whitewashed wood made it seem timeless.

The garage next to it was far newer, but no less charming. The top was wood painted a tidy white. Cornflower blue batten-board shutters bracketed the windows in the apartment upstairs. The foundation was stone. Solid, just like the lighthouse.

Just like Mason appeared to be.

As they pulled up the drive, Roz noticed a path of what looked to be cobblestones led from the door of the lighthouse to the garage. Snow had been neatly removed and piled high on each side of the walkway.

He parked in front of the garage and got out. She followed him up the narrow, snowy staircase that was attached to the side of the building, surprised when he didn't fumble for keys. Instead he just turned the knob. The door was unlocked and gave way with a rusty squeak of hinges. With one arm, he motioned for her to precede him inside.

Marnie hadn't been kidding about it being small. Small, dusty, full of mismatched furniture and decorating castoffs that dated back at least a few generations. And Marnie had been right. It was *perfect*.

"It's not much," Mason said, frowning as he glanced around the room.

Roz kept her expression neutral. She merely shrugged and set her duffel bag on the floor just inside the door.

"I've lived in worse."

Much, much worse. Even with perfectly matched furniture and not a dust bunny in sight, homes could be really ugly, Roz knew.

"Electricity's on, and I'll have to turn on the water. Bathroom's through there," he said, motioning to one of only two doors in the place. The other, Roz assumed, belonged to a closet. "I'd advise you to let the water run for a while before showering or drinking. We've got plenty of, um, iron content around here," he said, wrinkling his nose.

That, she assumed, was his fancy way of saying the water smelled like rotten eggs.

"You'll need to arrange for phone service."

"No need," she shrugged. "I've got no one to call."

"Oh, well..." He rubbed his hands together and moved over to the thermostat, turning it up until she heard a furnace blower kick on. "Since Marnie's not here yet, I'll give you a hand cleaning up."

"That's not necessary."

She should have known he wouldn't listen to her.

"I've got some cleaning supplies at the house. I'll be back in a minute."

When the door clicked behind him, Roz let the grin come. Then she laughed out loud, happier than she could remember being in a very long time. Of course, she wouldn't be staying long, she reminded herself. She'd be pulling up stakes as soon as she raised enough cash for some rusty, but reliable transportation.

For the first time, the idea of heading out on the open road held no appeal. She went to the window and couldn't help wondering if the dark-haired man who was slipping in the door of the lighthouse had something to do with that.

Bergen was in the kitchen when Roz entered the Lighthouse Tavern by the back door at the start of her shift that evening. She wore one of the shirts Mason had given her and a pair of jeans that were faded but clean. And she was as freshly scrubbed as her new apartment, having enjoyed the luxury of a long, hot shower before coming to work.

The cook grunted something at her that might have been hello when she poked her head into the kitchen.

"Mason said I could find an apron in here," she said, cautiously eyeing the large knife the man used to chop onions. She took a small amount of satisfaction from noting that they were making his eyes tear.

"Clean ones are hanging on a peg over there."

He motioned with the knife in the general direction of the far wall. Despite the Ginsu he held in one gnarled hand, Roz couldn't help teasing him. "Tears of joy, hmm. Who knew you'd be so happy to see me."

A full stomach, a good-paying job and a roof over her head must have made her cocky. Bergen, however, didn't share her enthusiasm.

Roz swore he was pointing the lethal five-inch blade at her heart when he said, "Pay no mind to my blurry vision, girlie. I've got my eye on you."

It wasn't anything she hadn't heard before, and sometimes, Roz could admit, for good reason. She'd pulled her share of cons, done her share of fast-talking when the situation called for it. She wasn't a liar or a cheat by nature, but it was hard to live by some high moral code when you had an empty belly or frostbitten feet. So she'd lied at times, stolen at times, although always out of need rather than greed. Roz found that shade of gray acceptable, if uncomfortable. But standing before Bergen, she doubted he would agree. She also doubted he would believe her if she told him she would never con Mason or Marnie. They had been too kind to her to deserve anything less than her honesty and hard work.

''Clock's ticking,'' he said, one wiry eyebrow winging upward.

Roz snagged an apron and left the kitchen without another word.

By nine o'clock the Lighthouse Tavern was hopping, with patrons standing three deep at the bar and every table occupied. Roz swore the entire population of Michigan's Upper Peninsula had turned out for Bergen's fish and chips special. The first couple dozen times she'd served it, the flaky battered lake trout had made her mouth water. Now she was wondering if she would ever get the smell out of her clothes.

Marnie, who was filling in for the other nightshift waitress who was still sick with the flu, looked just as harried as she felt. Mason, however, was tending bar and doing it so expertly, he hardly looked busy. She took a moment to appreciate the competent way he mixed a drink and made conversation at the same time with a couple of older men who sat perched on high stools.

She rounded the bar, sneaking a handful of beer nuts as she went.

"I need three drafts, two shots of Jack and a white wine spritzer," she told him. She tossed back the nuts and leaned against the bar. Roz was no stranger to hard work, but her feet were begging for relief. She thought about the couch that pulled out into a bed waiting for her back at her new digs and tried not to dwell on the fact that she still had at least four hours before she could call it a night.

"White wine spritzer? Who ordered that?"

"Only woman in the place wearing a suit."

He craned his neck, glancing around the crowded room until he spotted her.

"She your accountant or something?" Roz asked.

"I wish," he muttered. "She's the head of the state Democratic Party. I'll bet Marnie knows something about this."

She didn't get a chance to ask him what the woman was doing here or why Marnie would invite her. Any further conversation was obscured by the loud squawk of a fiddle as a country song blasted through the bar.

When the din died down somewhat, Mason groaned, "No Saturday evening would be complete without the Battle brothers monopolizing the jukebox. Hope you like hard-core country, 'cause if it ain't got a twang, it ain't playing for the next three hours."

She watched Mason grimace and sympathized. Three hours was an awfully long time for a die-hard rocker to have to listen to ballads about truckers and cheatin' wives.

An idea formed. "I get a break, right?"

"A break?"

"Fifteen minutes, that's all I need," she said, pulling off her apron.

He glanced up from loading the beverages on her tray. "For what?"

"To make you incredibly happy."

She winked when she said it and Mason felt his mouth go dry. "Fifteen minutes?" he repeated inanely.

He wanted a lot longer than fifteen minutes, he thought, as he watched her deliver the drink order to the table closest to the door and then slither through the crowd. He lost her a couple of times, but then she emerged near the pool table, where she grinned innocently at Brad and Brice Battle, two big hulking men who worked road maintenance for the county.

Mason would have given his eyeteeth to hear what she said to the smitten-looking duo. They appeared docile as kittens as they grinned their foolish aw-shucks grins. Before he could ponder their conversation overmuch, though, Rose was picking up a cue.

Curiosity got the better of him. He abandoned the bar and made a beeline to where she stood, nonchalantly applying blue chalk to the end of her stick.

"What are you doing, Rose?" he asked.

"I'm on break." She divided a slow grin between the men that had Mason's stomach doing a funny tumble. "Can't a girl have a little fun when she's off the clock, boss?"

"Come on, Mase, she's on her own time," Brice whined.

She counted out twenty dollars from her tip money and laid it on the edge of the table.

"You're playing him for money?" Mason asked incredulously. Pulling Rose aside, he said, "You can kiss that twenty goodbye. He's good. They both are."

Her lips never bowed, but Mason got the feeling she was smiling when she replied, "I'm better."

"You can break," Brice offered.

"Thank you," she said politely, and sent Mason a wink. She pocketed three balls on the break, two striped and one solid.

Walking around the table in her slow, sinuous way, she reminded him of a cat stalking prey.

"Solid," she said, to which Brice looked pleased.

If there was a reason behind the choice, Mason didn't see it. He could count at least three easy shots to be made with striped balls.

"Why solids?" he asked when she walked to where he stood near one of the corner pockets of the pool table.

She contemplated her next shot before answering, and when she did Mason witnessed her transformation from innocent young barmaid to hustling pool shark.

Chalking her cue, she said, "I had to do something to make it challenging."

That said, she got down to business. She wasn't one to overcontemplate a shot. She walked around the table in her leggy swagger, made her choice of ball and pocket, and then took her shot. Mason supposed her confident strategy only worked so well because Rose was that good. She didn't miss as one after another of the solid balls disappeared down the holes like rabbits being chased by a fox. Mason felt his mouth drop open as she pulled off some of the fanciest stick work he'd ever seen in his bar or any other.

Finally, with just the eight ball left, she called the corner pocket where Mason stood. Even in this, she made the task more difficult than it needed to be. The side pocket would have been the smarter choice, a little nudge with the cue ball and it would be in. But, of course, there was no challenge in that. She leaned over the table and lined up the shot, but for the first time, she hesitated. With a slow, sexy sweep of lashes, she shifted her gaze to Mason and she didn't break eye contact as she pulled back the stick and then pushed it forward in one fluid movement. The eight ball was sliding into the corner pocket before she looked away and Mason realized he'd been holding his breath the entire time.

She walked around the table to him, smiling as she came. She's not beautiful, he thought, inventorying her angular features and spiky dishwater-blond hair. Yet something seemed to sizzle in the air, more potent than the whiskey the Battle brothers were consuming to commiserate their loss.

"I told you I was better."

She picked up her money and dropped it back into the pocket of her apron.

"Pleasure playing you, Brice."

"Hey, wait a minute," Mason called when he recovered the power of speech. Pointing to Brice, he said, "He never paid up."

She sent him a smile over one slim shoulder as she walked away. "He will."

Mason was back behind the bar drawing drafts for a group of snowmobilers when he heard Springsteen's gritty voice belting out the singer's origin of birth.

"What the..." His gaze swung to the jukebox in time to see a none-too-pleased Brice Battle plunking in more quarters. From across the crowded bar, he caught Rose's Cheshire cat grin. So, this was the payoff.

For the next couple of hours, as songs ranging from heavy metal to vintage rock rolled from the jukebox, Mason found himself ever more appreciative of Rose's stellar ability with a cue stick.

Just after two o'clock, Mason waved the last of the regulars out the door. He flipped the locks when they were gone and turned on the overhead lights, exposing the filthy floor and sticky tables.

Marnie shook her head.

"You prefer this to rubbing elbows with the state's movers and shakers?"

Mason glared at her, but said nothing, so Marnie addressed Roz.

"He should be putting together an election committee and having fund-raisers so he can run for the Michigan Legislature fall after next. The chairwoman of the state party drops in tonight and what does he tell her? He'd rather pour drinks and sweep floors than be a candidate for public office."

Roz didn't particularly want to get into the middle of something she wasn't completely sure she understood. What she did know, though, was that Mason didn't want to talk about it. She'd honor that wish. He'd been too kind to her for her to consider doing otherwise.

"Heads you clean the bathroom, tails I do."

She plucked a quarter from her apron pocket and tossed it in the air. After a little sleight of hand, she said, "Sorry, Marnie, looks like you're scrubbing toilets."

When she was gone, Mason grinned, apparently aware of the con. "Thanks, I owe you."

Rose shrugged and began counting out her tip money. From the size of the stack of bills, it looked as if she'd had a very good night. Of course, she could have made another twenty dollars if she'd played Brice for money instead of jukebox rights.

Mason figured he owed her for that, too.

"Hey, why don't you take a load off your feet. I'm feeling rejuvenated by three hours of quality music. I'll sweep and mop the floor and tackle the tables. It won't take me long, then we can be on our way."

"You're right. It won't take long, because I'll help." She repocketed her tip money and picked up a bleach-soaked rag. If she was tired, it didn't show as she began to vigorously wipe down the tabletops.

A few minutes later Mason called, "Hey, I found two quarters."

"Must be your lucky night. Now you can put on some more head-banging music." She stopped wiping a table and leaned against it instead. "You know, I think guys only like that music 'cause it gets them out of dancing."

"I like to dance."

She eyed him speculatively. "Yeah, sure. I can see you shakin' it like Ricky Martin."

"Please. I said I like to *dance*."

Mason told himself he was only interested in wiping that amused look off her face when he deposited one of the quarters in the jukebox and pressed G-19. As Selena's whispery words filled the smoky room, he walked to Rose and extended a hand.

"What?" She looked wary, nervous. That gave him courage. If she'd been standing there with that smirk, still mocking him, he doubted he would have had the nerve to reach out and pull her into his arms. Their hips bumped together and she stumbled back a step.

"Mason, I don't..."

"Don't dance?" he finished for her. "Then let me show you how."

He settled her into his arms, enjoying the feel of her even if he did think she could use a few extra pounds to round off the angles.

"There's nothing to it, really. It's easy."

Easy? Roz thought as she stepped on his toes and knocked into his knees with her own. She felt gangly rather than graceful, but Mason persisted, talking her through the steps.

"Three forward and one back. It's basic, but it beats going around in circles with your arms draped all over each other like seventh-graders at their first boy-girl dance.''

Roz didn't tell him, but she'd never been to a dance as a seventh-grader or otherwise. Still, she had an idea of what he was talking about. She'd worked in enough bars to watch men and women shuffling around with the precision of a drill bit while locked in a seemingly unbreakable embrace.

So that he wouldn't think she was counting out the steps—which she was—she asked, ''Where'd you learn to dance?''

''My grandmother on my mother's side. She insisted Marnie and I learn, so whenever we went downstate to visit with her, she'd put on some Perry Como or Frank Sinatra, and we'd spend at least an hour learning the dance moves she swore Grandpa used to woo her.''

''Woo?'' she chuckled at the old-fashioned word.

''Haven't you ever been wooed?''

''I'm not sure.''

He dipped her low and brought her back up slowly. ''What about now?''

Her heart knocked clumsily, and before she could think better of it, she replied, ''Did you say wooed or wowed?''

"I get the two confused myself," he said with a laugh.

"So, Grandma taught you to dance."

"Actually, this little bit of footwork is my own, but I give her credit for my fox-trot, cha-cha and box-step waltz."

"A man of many talents," Roz said, and then apologized as she stepped on his toes once again.

She liked the way he held her. It was as old-fashioned as the word woo, with his right hand resting lightly on the small of her back and his left hand loosely clasping her right one. Their bodies were barely touching, just a brush of contact here and there as Selena sang of how she could fall in love.

"This song is so sad," Roz sighed and surprised them both when, just for a moment, she rested her head on his shoulder.

"Why do you say that? It's about possibilities. Do you think falling in love is something to be sad about?"

"I wouldn't know."

"No?" He eased her back a little so he could look her in the eyes.

"I've never been in love." She watched

his mouth as she said it. He really did have a very nice mouth.

"Then why do you think this song is sad?"

"The singer died violently. She was just starting to realize her dream when someone ended her life. Every time I hear this song, I think of her and wonder how many other great songs she might have sung if she were still alive. It makes me sad."

"Well, here's something else you can think about the next time you hear this song."

Mason wasn't sure where the impulse came from, but it was too strong to resist, so he dipped his head and settled his mouth over hers. She went still in his arms, but she didn't pull away, so he tilted his head and deepened the kiss. Her muscles went lax and she leaned in closer, her small breasts resting against his chest.

Was that her heart thumping or his?

He didn't waste time trying to figure it out. He had more pressing business at the moment. He maneuvered her arms so they encircled his neck.

"Rose," he whispered against her lips.

Rose. She wasn't Rose. She was Roz.

Roz Bennett. And Roz Bennett would be leaving soon enough. There was no sense in getting involved with someone like Mason—someone who might make her want to stay—because in her vast experience, she had always been forced to leave.

She pulled away from him as Selena's song ended, and she knew she would remember this heart-stopping kiss with or without any musical prompting.

"I think I'll go see if Bergen needs a hand in the kitchen."

"Bergen doesn't need a hand," Mason said, blowing out a deep breath. "Rose, about—"

"My name is Roz."

"I know your name." There was a touch of impatience in his tone that surprised her.

"Then why do you keep calling me Rose?"

He shrugged his shoulders. "I don't know. It just seems to fit you better. Consider it a nickname."

"I have a nickname. It's Roz," she said stubbornly. She wasn't sure why she was arguing with him about this. She was clear in her own mind who she was. What she was. She supposed she just wanted to make sure he was clear about it as well.

"Who gave you that nickname?"

She glared at him. "You know who gave me my name."

"I know the state gave you the name Rosalind. Who started calling you Roz?"

His question pulled up memories as painfully as a tooth extraction without Novocain. She turned away, picked up the bleach-soaked rag and began wiping down another table with aggressive, restless swipes. Mason didn't touch her, but she felt him behind her, once again patient.

His voice was a whisper when he asked, "Who tagged you as a Roz?"

She moved on to another table without answering his question. At least out loud. In her mind, she remembered…and mourned.

Her original nickname had been Rosa, given to her by the first foster parents who took her.

"We'll be a family. You'll be our very own little Rosa," they'd promised each night as they'd tucked her in. Not everyone under their roof, however, had been quite so enthusiastic about making her stay permanent. At six she'd been "tagged" with the name Roz by the brutal boy who had smoked half a pack of cigarettes and stubbed each one of them out on her arm. His sadistic behavior ensured she was placed elsewhere. What else could her foster parents do but send her away? She was just the child they'd raised for three years and promised a home to. He was their biological son.

"It doesn't matter," Roz said. She put the rag back in its bucket behind the bar. "I'll go see if Marnie needs help in the rest rooms."

"Okay." He hesitated only a moment before adding, "Rose."

When she was gone, he sank down onto a chair and cursed himself for a fool. For a woman who traveled so light, he'd never met anyone with so much baggage. Steer clear, his head warned. Don't get involved. She wasn't his problem, even if he did feel compelled to keep reaching out to her.

It was just attraction. Hormones. That's why he'd kissed her. No crime there. No harm, either.

As long as it wasn't repeated.

CHAPTER FOUR

THEY didn't speak of the kiss on the short ride home that night or the next morning when he knocked on her door, steaming mug of coffee in one hand and a sheepish smile on his face.

"I thought I heard you moving around when I went in the garage to get the snow shovel. I brought you this." He handed her the mug. "I know you don't have a maker yet."

"Come on in," she said, hoping he wouldn't figure out that the sweats she wore were really her pajamas.

"It's a little chilly in here." He motioned to the thermostat. "Is the furnace working okay?"

"It's fine. I like things a little cool."

"Oh." He dipped his hands into the pockets of his jacket and stood just inside the door on the mat, looking as awkward as Roz felt.

"You want some..." Her voice trailed off as it dawned on her that she had nothing to give him.

Nothing at all.

She ran a hand through her hair, for the first time in ages wondering about her appearance.

"I don't have anything to offer in return for the coffee."

Silence followed her statement, which she knew summed up more than the contents of her kitchen cupboards.

"But, thanks."

"There's more where that came from," he said with a quick grin that melted some of the awkwardness and she swore it warmed the room by a degree or two as well. "A whole pot, as it happens. Why don't you get yourself together and come on over for some breakfast. Later, I'll take you into town so you can get some groceries."

Because she liked just a little too much the idea of spending the day with him, she said, "I'm sure you have better things to do on a Sunday than cart me around the Shop-and-Save."

"You're right. We'll go to church first."

He winked and was gone, leaving her to wonder if he really expected her to attend Sunday services.

Roz had taken a shower after work the night before, so she only had to wash her face and brush her teeth. Looking in the mirror, she glanced at the spiky mess of hair on top of her head and scowled. Just for a moment she recalled what it had looked like long. She'd worn it all one length and past her shoulders when she'd had a permanent place to stay. Relying on public rest rooms to perform personal hygiene tasks had convinced her to chop it off and to give up her makeup bag as well. Besides, living on the road, all that hair had only drawn attention to her, the unwanted variety that no woman in her right mind courted.

After one last glance at her reflection, she pulled on jeans and a clean T-shirt, grabbed her coat and the mug of coffee, and walked down the stairs Mason had so thoughtfully cleared of snow.

They'd gotten another two inches overnight. Roz knew the snowmobilers and cross-country skiers would be thrilled. Since she didn't have to walk or drive in it or heft a shovel, she took a moment to admire the beauty of all that pristine white blanketing Superior's rocky shoreline as well as evergreen boughs beneath a sky so blue and clear it almost hurt the eye to look at it.

"Pretty, isn't it?" Mason said.

He watched her jump at his softly spoken words and winced. He hadn't intended to startle her. He'd thought she'd seen him in the yard adding seed to his bird feeder, which had already attracted a rowdy crowd of black-capped chickadees.

A look of wonder had been on her face as she'd regarded the landscape, and in that unguarded moment, she'd been utterly beautiful.

"Come on in." He walked ahead of her and opened the door to the lighthouse.

He left his snow-covered boots on the mat just inside the door and hung his down coat on a peg, then reached back to take Rose's coat. It was too thin for the weather. It wouldn't protect her from the wind's bite or the snow's damp chill. She wore shoes, sneakers that were well-worn on their white soles. As she hunched over to untie the dingy laces, he realized she probably didn't own boots. When she straightened, he noticed her socks were so thin that one large toe stuck out the end. He'd never known poverty, but he knew what it looked like. And yet Rose didn't act as if anything were owed to her, even as her holey socks obviously embarrassed her.

"Nice place," she said as she followed him into the tiny kitchen.

"Thanks. It's small with postage-stamp-sized closets, odd-shaped rooms and only one john, but like I said, you can't beat the view."

He motioned to the wide window and she knew he was right. She was a woman who always tired of her surroundings and gave in to the itch to move on. But this view...she didn't think such breathtaking scenery would ever bore her.

She sat on one of the high stools on the opposite side of the counter that divided the small kitchen nearly in two. He stood on the other side and flipped on the front burner of a gas range.

"Eggs okay? I'm not much of a cook, but I can do scrambled."

"As long as there are no beer nuts in

them, eggs will be fine. Was that window always here?''

He glanced to where she pointed and then refilled her mug with coffee and poured himself a cup. As he mixed eggs and milk in a bowl, he said, ''A smaller version of it, yes. I've done some updating.''

In truth, he'd done more than update. He'd gutted the entire lighthouse and replaced everything, adding oak floors throughout, new light fixtures, cabinets and bigger windows.

''So, you grew up in Chance Harbor?'' Roz looked slightly awed by the notion, and he realized it would be a foreign concept for her to willingly spend so much time in one place.

''Yep. Fought with Marnie every morning over bathroom rights at our folks' house until I went to college.''

''College, huh?'' She sounded almost glum. ''What did you get a degree in?''

''Criminal justice.''

''That's an odd major for a bar owner, isn't it?''

He shrugged. ''But not for a cop.''

"Cop?"

"Six years, Detroit. And I did some investigative work after that."

"Mason Striker, P.I.," she murmured, sipping her coffee. "Sounds like a television series."

It had had none of the glamour of TV. But then, he knew better than most people how grim reality could be. Not all of it had been bad, of course. But neither had it been glamorous. Most days he'd spent on the telephone or in his car, looking for answers. Legwork was a big part of the business. Following up leads, talking to sources.

It wasn't particularly dangerous work, either. Unless you got careless.

Unless you were lied to.

"I think those eggs have been beaten enough," she said.

It took him a moment to realize that he had whisked them into a pale yellow froth. He flipped on the burner and poured the mixture into a frying pan.

They ate in silence, with Roz wondering what it was that had so soured Mason's mood.

*   *   *

Just after noon, they pulled into the parking lot of a small, whitewashed church that boasted arched stained-glass windows and the traditional steeple. It was lovely, postcard perfect. It was Roz's worst nightmare.

"I can't go in there," she said as Mason began to open his door.

"You don't have to be Catholic to attend."

She rolled her eyes. The man didn't have a clue.

"I can't go in a church," she persisted. "Look how I'm dressed."

Look at who I am, she thought.

"How you dress isn't important. God won't hold it against you."

These were easy words for a man wearing khaki pants and a clean sweater. Easy words for a man who had never sat huddled under some highway overpass or tucked into some filthy doorway cursing his creator or questioning God's very existence.

"It'll be fine, I promise," he said as he opened her door and took her hand. "We'll sit in the back. No one will even notice us."

No one will notice us? Roz swore the entire congregation stopped midhymn when they entered. At the very least, a few notes were missed, replaced by whispers and certainly stares. This might have had something to do with the fact that the door through which Mason entered was at the side of the church and opened not far from the altar.

"I thought you said we'd sit in the back?" she hissed through her teeth as she met the dozens of curious gazes.

"We will, but we're late."

He nodded in the direction of a robed man who was at that very moment walking slowly up the center aisle along with other somber-looking people, all of whom seemed to be carrying something. Roz might not be Catholic, but she knew enough to figure out the man was a priest and Mass had already begun.

They hurried down the side aisle, past row after row of occupied pews. It didn't dawn on Roz till Mason stopped at the last row and executed a funny little bow on one knee that he still held her hand. He released it to make the sign of the cross. Roz followed everything he did and tried to duplicate it or at least not draw any more attention to herself. She thought she was getting the hang of the stand and sit thing when kneeling was thrown in.

The tunes the organist painstakingly played weren't the hand-clapping numbers she recalled from attending Baptist services with foster family number three. Still, there was something moving about the words of one song in particular. She liked the idea of being lifted up on eagle's wings. It sounded, well, heavenly. She found herself humming it after the Mass ended and they made their way outside.

Several people greeted Mason by name as he passed, offering him handshakes and friendly pats on the back, giving her a curious once-over or hesitant smile and then a polite hello when he introduced her. And he introduced her to each and every one of them.

"This is Rose Bennett. She's new in town and working at the tavern."

His words were truthful and yet they made her feel like a fraud, and certain a well-aimed lightning bolt would strike her down at any moment.

Marnie was standing next to Mason's car and grinning foolishly when they reached it. Something passed between the siblings, an indecipherable look that left sister pleased and brother scowling.

"I didn't know you were Catholic," she said to Roz.

"Neither did I."

"I didn't know you attended noon services," Mason said, his tone almost accusing.

"Hal and I didn't get up early enough this morning to make it at ten," Marnie shrugged casually, although the feline smile curving her lips had newlywed written all over it. She addressed both of them when she asked, "What's on your agenda for today?"

"I thought I'd take Rose to the grocery store, maybe catch the Packers game."

"Gosh, Mase, you sure do live on the edge on your day off," Marnie teased.

The reminder that Sunday was the only day the tavern closed made Roz feel uneasy about monopolizing any more of it than she already had.

"You know, Mason, you really don't need to run me to the store. It's not that far and I don't plan to buy much. I can walk. It's a nice day."

Both siblings looked at her as if she'd

grown a second head. But Mason only said patiently, "I'll take you to the store."

A few minutes later, he dropped her at the front of the Shop-and-Save and promised to be back within the half-hour.

"I'll just be at the gas station down the road. I want to get my Jeep washed and refilled."

By the time Mason returned twenty minutes later, Rose was heading in the direction of the register. He noticed her right away when he entered the store. She stuck out like a sore thumb, tall and thin as she was, and wearing clothes that would have been impractical in the city in winter, but were downright foolhardy in a town battered by lake-effect snowstorms.

He hadn't been trying to make her less self-conscious when he told her not to worry about wearing her faded jeans and thinly insulated denim jacket into church. God really didn't care about clothing. But the Almighty, Mason knew, was a lot less picky than Mother Nature when it came to one's wardrobe.

He watched her unload her purchases on the conveyor belt at the checkout. There wasn't much, half a dozen cans of fruits and veggies. A loaf of bread. Butter. Eggs. Milk. Instant coffee and, what he considered her one bow to her taste buds, a bag of red licorice whips. And just as he had inventoried her groceries, he did so to her features, again trying to figure out why it was he found her so attractive.

It certainly wasn't her hair. It stuck out at odd angles and made Meg Ryan's messy 'do look neat by comparison. Although he'd be lying if he said that it hadn't grown on him. She wore no makeup, not even a sweep of blusher on her pale, but prominent cheekbones. And the edgy, wary way she moved, as if always girding for some attack, certainly didn't encourage a man's lust, but put all together, for some reason they did encourage Mason's.

He closed his eyes and sighed as he felt the kick of it again now. At least it's just lust, he thought. Hormones he could deal with. It was his heart that had gotten him into so much trouble the last time.

"Almost done," she called when she spotted him. He watched the wariness recede, replaced by a hesitant smile, and he felt his already jumping pulse go off like a bottle rocket.

He was a sucker for vulnerable women, that's all it was, he assured himself again. He probably suffered from that White Knight Syndrome he saw some television talk show host discuss with a shrink on her show. As she stood in profile to him, he watched her dip her hands into the front pockets of her jeans, pulling them tight across her bottom, and knew there was nothing chivalrous about his thoughts.

He joined Rose at the checkout lane, offering a nod of greeting to the cashier, Penny Lindman. Mason had gone to school with Penny. The sallow-skinned brunette had been pretty then, but that was fifty pounds, three kids and two husbands ago. Now she was just a bitter and lonely woman who liked to stick her nose into everyone else's business. Living in a small town made her avocation easy.

"Hey, Mason, this is a surprise." Speculation lit her eyes and he could all but see her mentally rubbing her hands together as she split her gaze between him and Rose.

"Hey, Penny. How are the kids?"

"Fine, fine." She waved away his question as if eager to get on to a juicier topic.

"I didn't realize this here was a friend of yours."

Although he didn't really want to, Mason introduced the two women. From the amused look on Rose's face, he could tell she had already pegged Penny as a busybody.

"You must be new in town. Are you the gal Mason hired to replace Carol?"

And so the inquisition began, Mason thought with an inaudible sigh.

"Yeah."

"Where are you from? Originally, I mean."

"Detroit."

"Oh, the city, eh?" Penny's tone filled with pity, an emotion that didn't quite reach her eyes, and said, "I didn't think Mason here would date another gal from the city, not with what happened the last time."

Rose shot him a questioning look, but before he could speak she said, "We're not dating."

Penny pursed her lips, clearly unconvinced, but said nothing.

"How much do I owe you?" Rose asked.

The entire order came to less than twenty dollars and fit in a single brown paper bag. Rose didn't carry a purse. She was the only woman Mason had ever met who didn't. Most, in his experience, hefted ones the size of carry-on luggage and he'd wondered more than once exactly what they stowed in them. But Rose reached into the front pocket of her jeans again and pulled out her money, carefully peeling off two tens to hand to the cashier.

As Penny counted back Rose's change, she said, "So, you're not dating Mason?"

"Nah." Leaning in closer, Rose added in a confidential whisper, "I'm living with him."

"I can't believe you told her that," Mason murmured as he loaded her groceries into the Jeep. He'd insisted on carrying the bag. Of course.

He glanced back at the store. "She's probably already called half the town and, believe me, her dialing finger is just getting started."

Roz wasn't sure why she'd said it, but she was already regretting it. She didn't have anything to lose with the glib comment. She'd be moving on soon enough. But Mason had to live here, had to deal with the rumors and whispers that Roz had always tried to stay one step ahead of with her nomadic ways.

"Have I hurt your reputation?" she asked, seriously, contritely.

"Are you kidding?" He walked up behind her and spun her around so fast her feet skidded in the slush. Before she could lose her balance, he grabbed her by the shoulders. It wasn't anger she saw on his handsome face, but male interest—basic, primitive, potent.

"I can think of worse reasons for a guy to become the talk of the town than for people to assume he's sleeping with his pretty new waitress."

Pretty?

Roz didn't often hear that word in reference to herself. She decided that was why her chest felt tight, why her pulse had begun to pound.

And she blamed it for what happened next.

Rising to her toes she stood nearly eye to eye with Mason. Roz had been kissed before—by Mason in fact, not twenty-four hours earlier. But *she* had never kissed anyone.

Only rarely did she initiate physical contact of any variety, from the platonic to the passionate. His eyes were as dark and delicious as Hershey's syrup, and she watched them widen fractionally as he figured out her intent. From her school days, she recalled a teacher reciting some line about eyes being the windows to the soul. She'd thought it a bunch of blather back then, and the idea certainly hadn't intrigued her enough to seek help with her studies. She'd stayed firmly entrenched in the crack of semiliteracy into which she had fallen.

But Mason's eyes were windows to something. His soul? Perhaps, and if that were the case, she decided his soul was beautiful. But it was more than that. He seemed to see Roz as she wanted to be, rather than as she was. Somehow, he saw a softer, more feminine, more refined version of the scrapping survivor she had become.

He saw a woman whom he called Rose.

Gratitude, that's all it was, she decided as she poured herself into the kiss, relying on instinct, trying for finesse. She brought her hands up to frame the hard planes of his face, and leaned in so that their bodies brushed and then molded through denim and down.

She could have stood there kissing him all day in the frozen parking lot had a car horn not blasted. Dazed, she pulled away, and vaguely heard Brice Battle holler something from the open window of his truck before he pulled it to a spot a few parking spaces over. His comment about their public display was both off-color and on-target.

Ninety degrees separated vertical and horizontal, but in that burst of passion, she'd contemplated the delicious slide from one position to the other—an audience, slushy asphalt and freezing temperatures be damned.

And it hadn't been all one-sided. Her face grew warm as she recalled how Mason's hands had strayed from her shoulders to the small of her back and then settled on her hips, applying a delicious kind of pressure as he'd pulled them forward. Last night, he'd been old-fashioned in the way he'd danced her around the room.

There was nothing old-fashioned about the way he held her now.

How long had it been since she'd blushed? She felt the heat creep up her neck, enflame her cheeks even as a bitter wind whipped out of the west. When she would have walked away, Mason took hold of her hand and tugged her back.

"You've got to stop worrying about my reputation," he teased. Then his expression sobered. "That was nice, Rose."

Roz didn't say anything, she couldn't. Written or spoken, words had always been her foe. And they failed her now, none seeming worthy enough to describe her emotions, her thoughts or the way a simple meeting of lips could make her yearn for basic things like a home and family.

Love.

Impossible things that had eluded her for more than two decades, even though at one time she had sought them out desperately.

He brought her hand to his lips and kissed the back of it just above her knuckles. The gesture was chivalrous, gentlemanly, and for some reason it made her feel unworthy as she stood there in her worn and ragged clothes.

Mason watched the emotions play across her face: vulnerability, need and a kind of sadness that puzzled him. That he could see them at all told him the kiss had affected her enough to let her guard down. A man without a conscience might have pressed his advantage at that point. But a man with a conscience and whose last encounter with the opposite sex had put his heart through a meat grinder, wisely retreated.

Keep it light, he told himself. It doesn't have to mean anything.

"Your hands are cold," he said. Opening the truck's passenger door for her, he added, "We've got to get you some warm gloves."

Mason insisted on carrying her bag for her when they reached home.

"I'm not an invalid," she muttered as she followed him up the steps, but secretly she was touched by his good manners. Most of the men she had encountered in the past several years would have considered using a napkin rather than their shirt-sleeve out of the question.

To their surprise, Roz had company. Marnie sat on the sofa reading a paperback, which she stowed in her oversized purse when they entered. She stood and stretched, her movements fluid and graceful.

"I wondered when you two would get back."

"What are you doing here?" Mason asked. "You know, it's impolite to barge into someone's place uninvited and just make yourself at home."

She waved away his comment, but sent Roz an apologetic smile. "Sorry. I didn't think you guys would take so long at the grocery store."

"You could have waited in my house," he noted sourly.

"I could have. But I came to see Rose, not you." She turned and pointed to a couple of large shopping bags next to the sofa. "I cleaned out my closets and I was thinking maybe there would be a few things you could use. I know we're not exactly the same size, but..." She shrugged.

Roz wanted to be embarrassed at such an obvious attempt at charity. She wanted to refuse politely or perhaps even with a little indignation. Instead she almost drooled. New clothes. There was bound to be something in the two large bags that fit her well enough that she could set fire to the garments she was wearing. And she would. With glee.

"Let me just put the groceries away," she said, trying for nonchalance. When she turned, Mason was grinning.

"Do I get to stay for the fashion show?"

Marnie answered before Roz could. "No. But you can come back in an hour with a couple of cans of cola, diet for me, and two nice BLTs." She walked over and patted his cheek. "Remember, low-cal mayonnaise on mine and I prefer whole wheat."

He grumbled all the way out the door.

When the latch clicked behind him, Marnie began pulling clothes from the bags: slacks, sweaters, jeans, blouses, even a pair of low-heeled black leather boots.

"What do you want to try on first?"

Roz quickly stowed her meager supplies in the cupboards and small refrigerator. "Are you sure you want to part with all of this? Some of this stuff looks barely worn."

"Some of it *is* barely worn," Marnie said with a touch of regret. "They've been gathering dust in the skinny side of my closet waiting for me to lose a few pounds.''

"You want to *lose* weight?" Roz replied. "Why? I mean, at least no one would mistake you for a boy."

"Yeah, well, I've given up on the idea that I'll ever fit into those things again. I bought them while planning my wedding. I ate lettuce three times a day for a month just to be sure I would fit into that gown. And I did look great."

Marnie sighed dreamily before her expression turned cunning. "Okay, strip."

"Excuse me?"

"I'll look the other way if you're modest, but I thought we'd figure out what fits and what can be altered and go from there."

"Altered?" That sounded like it would cost money. At this rate, Roz would be lucky to save enough for a car before her next birthday.

But then Marnie said, "Nothing more complicated than a stitch here and there. I'm not that handy with a needle."

Roz relaxed a bit and allowed herself to enjoy the excitement of picking out new clothes, even if they were slightly used.

Her hands skimmed soft cottons and warm wools, before settling on a pair of stone-colored khakis. Marnie handed her a thick cable-knit turtleneck sweater the color of moss.

"This looks good with it, and I bet the color will look nice on you. It never did much for me. Even Hal said so, and you know men. They rarely comment on clothing unless it's lingerie."

Roz pulled the sweatshirt over her head and shucked off her jeans, eager to have something other than denim and fleece next to her skin for a change. As her head emerged from the neck of the sweater, she caught the look of horror on Marnie's face and braced herself for questions about the scars on her arm from the cigarette burns.

"Sweet Lord," Marnie whispered, sucking in a breath. Her gaze connected with Roz's then and her expression turned apologetic. "I'm sorry, sugar, but those panties and that bra must go. I think the Puritans wore sexier things. And judging from their condition, I'd say they date to Puritan times."

Roz snorted out a laugh. Leave it to a

fashion queen like Marnie to be offended by underwear.

"It's not like anyone sees them," Roz replied a touch defensively, although privately she knew the other woman had a point. They were god-awful ugly and dingy besides.

Marnie reached for her duffel-bag-sized purse and hauled out a couple of mail-order catalogs. She held one in front of her as if it were the Holy Grail. "Behold, the mother of all that is silky and sexy. I give you, *Victoria's Secret.*"

"You carry an underwear catalog around in your purse?"

"Believe me, if I don't get to this baby before my husband does, I never see it."

She flipped it open and Roz instantly understood why. She doubted more cleavage would be on display at Hugh Hefner's mansion. Every woman was ideally proportioned and pouting.

"This is a great bra, lots of support," Marnie informed her. Then her gaze slid to Roz's more meager bust line and she pointed to the bra on the opposite page.

"This one is sexy as they come and perfect for someone with a little less...up top.''

Roz had to admit, it was nice and it came in five shades ranging from pastels to darker hues with names such as burgundy and molasses. Compared to the white cotton slingshot she wore, and which had come in a box at some drugstore, this bra was infinitely more feminine. Maybe she'd order one or two when she got her first check. Then she spied the price. She could buy four slingshots for that amount.

''Marnie, these are a little beyond my budget. Do they have anything in, say, the ten-dollar range?''

''Oh, sure, they've got some nice panties for that.'' She flipped ahead several pages, then tapped her fingers on the image of a buxom blonde. ''I like the French cut the best. I think they minimize my hips, but you'd probably look great in the bikinis.''

Roz had never worried about how she looked in underwear. As long as they were clean and didn't ride up, she'd never really given them much thought. Still, these did look comfortable and, well, a little decadent. She'd splurge.

''How many come in the package?''

"The package?"

"For ten dollars."

"Oh, honey, that's what they cost each. Unless you buy four, then they knock off a couple bucks. See?" She pointed to the writing on the top of the page. Writing Roz couldn't read.

"I think I'll pass."

"Come on, Rose. Live a little. Underwear makes the outfit."

"How can they make the outfit? You wear it beneath your clothes."

Marnie's smile turned feline. "Yes, but you know they're there. And the knowing affects your attitude. It gives you confidence. It makes you feel sexy and so you are sexy."

"All that from a push-up bra and some fancy French underwear? *That's* Victoria's secret?"

"Simple but effective."

Roz glanced back at the catalog. "And profitable, too."

"Think of it as an investment in your femininity."

"My femininity isn't going to get me to Wisconsin, at least not without being arrested. I've got to save up for that car."

She stood and reached for the pants that she'd draped across the arm of the couch.

She was working up the zipper when the door opened and Mason stepped inside.

"Hey, Rose, I was thinking about going—" Even before he whirled away, she caught sight of his crimson face. "Jeez, sorry."

"Why didn't you knock, brother dear?" Marnie asked sweetly and then laughed as Roz smoothed down the hem of the sweater.

"You can turn around now."

A blush still tinted his face. His reaction should have amused Roz, but she found herself touched instead.

"I should have knocked."

"You should have," Marnie agreed. "Especially after reading me the riot act."

Mason ignored her. "I won't make a habit of just barging in." He glanced at his sister. "Neither of us will."

Roz waved away his apology and, to keep the moment from becoming more awkward, she said, "So, what do you think of my new outfit?"

Mason thought it looked terrific, although he thought he might have preferred the view he would have accidentally enjoyed if he'd come in a few minutes earlier.

He tried to clear his mind. "You look nice."

And she did. More than nice. The sweater complemented her tawny hair and pale complexion, and the pants, while a little loose, were a nice variation from what he suspected were the only two pairs of jeans she owned.

"Thanks." She seemed self-conscious suddenly. "So, what were you saying when you came in?"

"Oh, yeah. I was thinking about going cross-country skiing." He pointed out the window. "There's a trail that starts at the edge of the woods across from the tavern and then snakes back around to the main road. It's only about two miles and fairly easy even for a beginner."

"I don't have skis and what would I wear?"

"You can use Marnie's old skis. She never uses them anymore."

His sister stuck out her tongue at him.

"If God had intended for us to freeze our butts off just to get a little exercise he wouldn't have given us the Nordic Track."

Mason ignored her. "As for clothes, you don't need to dress overly warm. Maybe add some long johns. What have you got on beneath that sweater?"

"Under my sweater?" she repeated as Marnie fell into a fit of laughter.

Between giggles the other woman managed, "Trust me, brother dear, you don't want to know."

CHAPTER FIVE

Roz wasn't sure what made her agree to go cross-country skiing with Mason. It involved the outdoors, physical activity and a man from whom she had already determined she should keep her distance given the strange way he pulled at her. Yet, she'd readily accepted his invitation, telling herself it was the lure of clearing her head in the cold air rather than spending more of the day with Mason that influenced her decision.

After a light lunch, she found herself with a pair of thin skis strapped to the bottoms of her feet, two long poles in her hands, wearing a borrowed hat on her head, borrowed gloves on her hands, borrowed long johns under her sweatpants and one of the new wool sweaters Marnie had given her over it all. She was no fashion plate and ten minutes into the endeavor she concluded she also was no skier.

"Maybe I'll just head back and you can go on your own," she said from her prone position on the snow-covered trail.

Mason just grinned and offered her the end of his ski pole to pull her upright.

"You'll get the hang of it," he promised. "It's not that hard. It just takes coordination and a little practice."

"I'm short on both," she grumbled, struggling to right herself. She couldn't believe she was willingly putting herself through this humiliation, not to mention physical torture. Must be something in the water she thought, refusing to admit it might be something in the man.

"It's like playing pool. That takes concentration, especially until you get the feel for it."

"And practice," she added. "Lots and lots of practice. I've been playing pool for years."

"Okay, but it also takes concentration. Apply some of that mindset here. Visualize what it is you want to do in your head. Then make your movements fluid, but purposeful. It's about rhythm. Watch me again."

Mason turned and glided down the trail

several yards, a study in grace and economy of motion. A study in male perfection. He wore a pair of navy nylon jogging pants over what she assumed were long johns, and a patterned navy and white wool sweater. The red wool hat on his head was similar to the one Roz wore. Of course, she wasn't paying much attention to what was covering his head. Her gaze was occupied elsewhere. Hmm, she thought, watching the nylon fabric pull and relax with each stride.

"Notice how my legs move with my arms?" he called back to her.

"Oh, yeah. I'm noticing," she murmured. Then shook her head. Definitely something in the water.

He stopped and turned around, his gaze full of patience. "Now let's see you do it, Rose."

Roz blew out a breath and planted her poles in the snow just as Mason had showed her. "Ready or not," she mumbled to herself.

"That's it. Right, left, right, left," he coached as she made progress from point A to point B. She knew her movements remained jerky and tentative, but something clicked, and suddenly it all seemed to take far less effort. Half an hour later, she had the gliding motion down enough to begin to enjoy the scenery. It was the dead of winter and most trees were naked, but there were enough evergreens of varying sizes and descriptions to keep the landscape from being dull. In fact, it was downright beautiful.

"Is this your land?" she asked in awe as they skied beneath some of the largest pine trees she'd ever seen.

"No, the state owns it."

He stopped, leaned negligently against his ski poles and looked around with a satisfied grin. "Pretty, eh? I have to admit, I really missed this living in the city."

A shadow clouded his face then. He didn't talk much about his life in Detroit, she realized, changing the subject whenever Marnie brought it up. Something had happened there. Something bad. Roz wasn't one to pry, but she had to admit, she was curious.

"Did you live right in the city?"

He nodded. "East side when I was a cop. Later, when I became self-employed as an investigator, I rented a loft apartment not far from Greektown."

"What made you decide to leave?"

He positioned his poles as if to ski away, then relaxed his pose again.

"I got shot."

Of all the things he might have said, this surprised her the most. She was no stranger to the danger of the streets. And, as a cop and private investigator, he'd probably come into contact with more unsavory characters than she'd had the misfortune of meeting. But shot. Mason?

"Your shoulder?" she guessed, recalling the way he often rubbed it.

"Yep."

The curt answer told her to leave it alone, but she heard herself ask: "What happened?"

He glanced away, as if impatient to leave. But then he said, "I was hired by...someone important to keep his daughter safe. What the man didn't realize was that she had fallen into drugs. I followed her to a drug house on the city's east side, where she'd gone to buy a fix. Things...got ugly."

She doubted he realized how much his expression gave away despite his rather sanitized explanation.

''What happened to her?''

He shrugged nonchalantly but his lips thinned. ''Rehab out west, someplace where the celebrities go. Very discreet.''

''The important person who hired you didn't want any bad publicity,'' she guessed.

Mason nodded.

''And you. What did you want?''

''What do you mean?''

''You loved her, right?''

He started to shake his head, but said quietly, ''Yes, I loved her.''

''Did she love you?''

His expression turned bitter. ''She loved a fix. She loved defying her father. But, no, in the end it turned out that she didn't love me. Just as her father loved his reputation and keeping his position more than he cared about keeping her from harming herself. I hear she's back into drugs already.''

''Sorry, Mason.''

He waved off her pity with a lift of one pole and then used it to point down the trail.

''Let's ski.''

He was quiet after that, but Roz didn't take it personally. Still, her mind worked overtime, wondering about this woman Mason had loved and lost and taken a bullet for.

They reached the halfway point on the trail, or so Mason claimed. Roz's skill had improved enough that she had only fallen once more. Since the conversation remained limited, Roz paid more attention to the scenery. Rarely had she taken time to enjoy nature's beauty. Usually she was too busy trying to figure out where she'd be sleeping or how she could hustle up a meal. And certainly none of the men who had previously entered her social sphere had given two beans about the way snow lingered on barren tree boughs or glinted like a throw of diamonds on a hillside in the afternoon sunlight. But she took the time now and came close to sighing aloud.

"Does this tree have a name?" she asked, breaking the silence and pointing to one of the towering giants to her right.

"Joe," Mason replied, straight-faced.

And she was glad to see his good humor was restored.

"Very funny."

"It's an eastern white pine, you know, Michigan's state tree." When she just kept staring at him, he continued, "It was the backbone of our logging industry at one time. This one is probably a couple hundred years old, judging from the circumference of the trunk."

She watched him try to ring the trunk with his arms. He couldn't. She let her head tip back, let green boughs, white snow and the crystal blue of a cloudless sky fill her vision.

"I like it, the way its branches aren't symmetrical. There's beauty to be found in that little bit of imperfection," she mused, surprising even herself with the almost poetic observation.

When she glanced at Mason, prepared for some ribbing, his face was serious, his gaze penetrating.

"You're right, Rose. Sometimes things are beautiful not in spite of their imperfections, but because of them."

Something about the way he smiled at her after he said it gave Roz goose bumps. But before she could reply, he skied away.

When they reached the road again, Mason used the end of his pole to unclip his boots from his skis.

"I'm going to stop in at the tavern for a bit."

"It's your day off," Roz said, feeling disappointed.

"I need to catch up on some paperwork."

"Oh."

She had skied a short distance when he called out, "I ski every day around ten. Clears my head before I go to work. You're welcome to join me."

Roz waved, but didn't commit. She didn't plan to take him up on the offer. She planned to steer clear of the water, or whatever else was responsible for her sudden interest in the great outdoors. But the next day she was out there, ready, if sore from the previous day's exercise. Again on Tuesday and Wednesday she strapped on the skis and followed Mason into the woods. And she no longer tried to deny or question why she was enjoying nature in a way she never had. That's because right along with the majestic pines and crisp country air, she was enjoying her first real taste of friendship.

*   *   *

A week went by and then two. Roz's life fell into a routine and yet she couldn't say she felt bored by it or itched to move on the way she always had in the past. Mason was teaching her to read, or rather trying to improve the limited skills she already had. It should have embarrassed her, she supposed, but he didn't make her feel stupid. Perhaps that's because his help had started innocently enough, with him making the offer in a way that left her pride intact.

"Hey, Rose," he said after her shift one night. "I picked up a couple of books at the library that I thought you might enjoy."

She glanced up, prepared to find him grinning at his cruel joke, but his face was serious.

"I know you don't read very well. I have a cousin who had the same problem when he was in school. Anyway, he recommended these books. I thought we might go over them together some time."

She shrugged noncommittally, but a couple of times a week after that, they sat hunched together behind the desk in his office for an hour before her shift. She didn't feel foolish sounding out the words or writing them down on paper. As a reward for her hard work, he read her a few pages at a time from one of his thick paperbacks. He had a great voice—steady, sure, the cadence and inflection just right to keep the story riveting. They were reading his favorite right now: *Last of the Mohicans* by James Fenimore Cooper.

With her chin propped in her hands and elbows on the desk, she asked, "This takes place in upstate New York, right?"

"Yes, but the British had installments in Michigan as well. Ever been to Fort Mackinac?"

When she shook her head he said, "We'll go some time."

He said it casually, the way one friend might to another, and it took all of Roz's willpower not to let her mouth gape open. How did he do that? she wondered. He had a knack for making her seem special, important, and she knew she was neither. Yet, when he spoke to her, he made eye contact. And when she talked, he didn't just make the appropriate noises, she knew he really listened.

She'd been invisible most of her life, showing up on other people's radar only when they thought she might be trouble.

She'd been anonymous as well, a number in the foster care system, whose sheer volume of children made interactions seem obligatory and impersonal. But Mason saw her. He made the time they spent together enjoyable and relaxed, if one didn't count her elevated pulse whenever he casually laid a hand on her shoulder or sent her a simple smile. And she had fun with him. Just like the reading lessons, which should have made her feel dumb, he made their ski outings about more than physical exertion.

Right along with improving at both pastimes, she'd gotten better at conversation. Mason fascinated her. Forget the Hollywood looks, intriguing past and the penchant for head-banging music, the man was a walking encyclopedia of knowledge when it came to nature and he was generous about sharing it. He could identify trees by their bark, tell her the type of animal that had walked the ski trail before them based on the tracks in the snow, and he was crazy about birds. Every now and then he would stop abruptly as they skied and cock his head to the side to listen to the shrill whistle or low peep of some feathered creature.

It was like skiing with the Crocodile Hunter. He showed that same brand of almost boyish enthusiasm and excitement for nature. Roz found it an endearing quality as well as a contagious one. And so on this morning as they skied what she considered the intermediate trail since it took them a mile farther from home, she decided to dazzle him with her own limited knowledge.

"Hey, hear that?" she asked.

He stopped just ahead of her and swiveled at the waist to look at her. "What?"

She waited until she heard the loud cry again. Overhead, a crow, black as midnight, flew through the overcast sky. She pointed.

"There. It's a crow. They like roadkill and garbage. They're found throughout the state and can be identified by their distinctive call and annoying table manners."

She tried to keep her expression serious, but the quivering of her lips gave her away.

"Smart aleck."

"You're not the only one who knows birds." She shrugged.

"I expect you're an expert on rock doves."

"Rock doves?"

He grinned and she knew she'd been had again.

"Better known as pigeons. Detroit had plenty of those. They're the city's unofficial mascot."

Caw-caw! The crow settled into the top of a nearby tree and shouted obscenely into the crisp, quiet air.

"The country's not that different from the city. You have noise pollution, too," Roz noted dryly, pointing with her ski pole.

"That we do. I heard someone say once that if a bird's call could be translated into English, while most would be reciting poetry, a crow would be cussing."

The big black bird squawked rudely again and Roz decided Mason had a point.

"Do you ever think of looking for your family?" Marnie asked as they cleaned up in the bar after closing time that night.

Roz shrugged nonchalantly. "Nah."

It was a lie, though. She may have given up on finding them, but she realized she was always looking. Each new place she visited, she scoured the faces of strangers seeking something familiar—a link, a connection, anything that would give her an identity beyond state-named Rosalind Bennett, case number 42577.

"I'd have to know. I wouldn't stop looking until I found out who they were and why they'd abandoned me," Marnie replied as she pressed fresh paper napkins into the table holders.

"Drop it, Marnie," Mason called from behind the bar.

But of course his pointed command didn't deter his sister.

"You could help her, Mase." She turned to Roz and added, "Mason's like a bloodhound. He could find the proverbial needle in a haystack. Did he tell you that he used to be a private detective?"

"He mentioned it," Roz said. She spared a glance at her boss. He was scowling at his sister.

"You still have contacts in Detroit, Mason. A few phone calls might be all it takes to get a decent lead."

"Marnie..." His tone held a warning, but as usual she waved it off.

"If you're going to hide out in Chance Harbor, you might as well do something useful with your time, like find Rose's family."

"Dammit, Marnie! Why do you always have to push things? Maybe Rose doesn't want her family found. Maybe I don't want to be reminded of..." He rubbed his shoulder, as if it pained him. As if the bullet he'd taken was still lodged there. "I left Detroit behind for a reason, you know. I'm not hiding out. I came back because I wanted to be around people who are real. You can trust folks here to say what they mean."

"It's a wonderful trait," Marnie agreed, not at all put off by her brother's display of temper. "One that's sorely lacking in the state Capitol building, whatever the political party. Honesty and integrity are old-fashioned values that never go out of style."

She smiled, apparently pleased with herself. "That could be your campaign slogan."

"God! You never quit!" Mason thundered. "First you're harping on me to dig into Rose's past and now you're plotting out an election strategy."

"Diane Sutherland from the Michigan Democratic Party thinks you're just what the ticket needs," his sister said calmly.

"And how would you know what Diane Sutherland thinks?"

Marnie shrugged. "I talked to her the other night when you were too busy pouring drinks to bother."

His expression turned stony. "I didn't invite her here. I'm a businessman, not a—"

"Public servant?" Marnie supplied.

"Public service," Mason scoffed. "That's a bunch of crap and you know it. Politics is a game. It's about special interests and the money they can provide for a candidate's reelection campaign. It's one big stinking power trip, with even the party coming in a distant second to personal ambitions. As for constituents, forget it. They only count on Election Day. It's not about helping people."

"But it could be. It *should* be," Marnie insisted. "And that's the kind of legislator you'd be. You would be a public servant, Mason. You wouldn't be just a politician."

"Would you quit already? I said stop pushing."

"Well, somebody needs to push you along," Marnie said tartly. She turned to Roz. "Both of you."

When Roz failed to rise to the bait, Marnie said, "You'd vote for him, wouldn't you, Rose?"

Oh, no. She wasn't going to be dragged into this one.

"I'm not a registered voter. I've never stayed in one place long enough to bother."

But Marnie was like a pitbull terrier with its teeth sunk into someone's backside.

"See there, Mase, you could be a champion for people like Rose. People who otherwise have no voice in our supposedly democratic society."

Muttering an oath, he tossed down the rag he'd been using to wipe up the bar and stalked to his office. After hearing the door slam shut, Marnie turned to Roz and winked.

"He's coming around," she said. "And I'm sure he'll agree to help you as well."

"I don't want his help," Roz said with an exasperated sigh. "I don't want to find…anyone."

She didn't let Marnie reply. Roz grabbed the mop and bucket and went into the kitchen, preferring dirty floors and

Bergen's not so subtle insults to Marnie's well-meaning pestering.

But that night, Roz thought about it. She lay awake on the pullout couch's lumpy mattress, watching the lighthouse's beacon strobe the inky sky, and wondered what she would say if she did find her mother.

Remember me?

What have you been doing for the past couple decades?

Have you missed me?

And the most burning question of all: *Why didn't you want me?*

CHAPTER SIX

THE sky was overcast and spitting little bits of jagged ice, but when Mason tapped on Roz's door on the last Sunday in February to see if she wanted to go for a ski, she eagerly agreed. The thought of sitting inside her apartment all day with no television, no radio and nothing to do but count the drips from the faucet Mason kept meaning to fix was enough to drive her insane.

An hour later, they were back, the biting snow stamping out any enthusiasm for the great outdoors. Mason had been especially laconic on the trail, so it surprised Roz that when they skied into his yard he invited her inside for hot chocolate. She almost declined, but her little apartment seemed empty and lonely compared to his lighthouse with its friendly beacon.

Once they had shucked off their gear, she settled onto one of the high stools in his kitchen and watched him prepare their drinks. She expected him to simply rip open two packets of powdered mix and add water that he'd nuked in the microwave. She supposed she should have guessed he would do things the right way, the old-fashioned way, the way that required patience.

He pulled out a saucepan from one of the lower cabinets and heated chocolate syrup-laced milk over medium heat. After rummaging through a couple of cupboards, he came back with two mugs and a bag of mini-marshmallows. She grabbed a handful of the marshmallows and munched while he stirred the heating milk.

"Are you hungry?" He turned after he said it and Roz stopped chewing and shook her head.

His gaze dipped to her mouth.

"Liar," he said softly.

He moved to the refrigerator, perfectly at ease in what many men would have considered a woman's room. Of course, a man on his own would have to know his way around a kitchen. He took out a plastic bowl and peeled back the lid for a sniff.

"Spaghetti's still good," he said. "I

made it for lunch a couple of days ago,'' he clarified when she arched a brow.

''You don't have to feed me.''

''There's enough here for two. I always make too much. Besides, my mother says it's rude to eat in front of people. I'd really like to eat right now, Rose, but I don't want to be rude. What do you say?''

''Well, when you put it that way.''

While he prepared the spaghetti for reheating, which of course was on the stovetop rather than in the microwave, Roz poured their hot chocolate, adding a generous heap of marshmallows to her own. The first sip she took after it had cooled somewhat left her top lip feeling sticky. Mason turned just as she was running her tongue over it. Something flickered in his eyes, and it was still there when he settled beside her at the counter.

He took a sip of his hot chocolate and stared at her over the rim of his mug for a moment, long enough to make her wonder what he saw.

Does he think my hair is too short? Too boyish? Too unstyled?

She hated herself for caring what he

thought of her appearance, but that didn't change the fact that she did.

Finally he said, "You know, Rose, I've got some red wine that would really complement that marinara a lot better than this hot chocolate."

Roz smiled. "Why not? I don't have to drive—or ski."

By the time the spaghetti was ready and had been topped with a little Parmesan cheese, Mason had poured the wine and set the small table. They ate in silence for a few moments, and then he set down his fork and gave her his full attention.

"I've been thinking about what Marnie said about helping you look for your family. And she's right—a pain in the butt, but right. I could make a few phone calls, start the ball rolling. That is, if you want to find them."

"I don't," Roz said. The reply was automatic, a well-honed defense mechanism that had never quite succeeded in keeping her from being hurt, she now realized.

Mason nodded and reached for his fork, but she laid one of her hands over his before he had a chance to pick it up again.

"I do. I want to look."

The words rushed out in a whisper and she glanced away after she said them. For some reason she couldn't fathom, tears stung her eyes.

Mason turned his hand over beneath hers, clasping her fingers and exerting enough pressure that she was forced to look at him again.

"It's okay," he said simply.

"But they didn't want me."

The words were out and they horrified her. She hated the weakness they represented.

"I want you, Rose." He seemed surprised after he said it, but he didn't take it back.

They were boss and employee, landlord and tenant. He had roots as deep and reaching as the trees that surrounded the Superior shore. She was like a tumbleweed, with no roots at all. Nothing good could come from tangling business with pleasure, friendship with a physical relationship. Nothing good at all.

"You're beautiful, Rose."

"I'm not."

"Calling me a liar?" he asked softly.

Then he stood and, still holding her hand, tugged her to her feet.

"I think the wine has gone to your head," she told him and smiled to keep the moment light. But he didn't smile back.

"I think you're afraid I'm going to kiss you again."

"Are you?"

He stepped forward, reached for her other hand and then settled both of them around his neck. Once his own hands were free again, he used them to frame her face.

"You'd better believe it."

She should make her excuses and leave, she thought, but she leaned in instead. And why not, she told herself. Consequences be damned. In that moment she fiercely wanted to stay, to belong somewhere and to someone. Maybe this was just a fantasy, but it felt good to imagine that this could be the place, that Mason could be the someone.

The kiss ended, but they didn't part. She'd never been very good at this ritual between men and women, but she decided to give flirting a try.

"It's warm in here."

After saying it, she waited barely a heartbeat before taking off her sweater, leaving her in one of his old long john shirts. There was nothing sexy about the baggy shirt, but she figured the message had been sent.

And received, she decided, when he replied, "Yeah. Hot."

After he said it, he pulled the sweater he wore over his head. Beneath it, he had on a thermal shirt that was a twin to the one he'd given her before their first skiing session. It looked different on him, hugging his broad chest and taut abdomen.

"What's for dessert, Mason?"

"What would you like?"

Okay, that put the ball squarely back in her court. Roz figured they might cautiously volley back and forth this way for the next several minutes in some sort of verbal foreplay, but she generally preferred actions to words.

"Well, I did like that kiss. Why don't we start with another...and then see where it leads?"

She didn't wait for him to initiate it. She kissed him. The tangy tastes of marinara and merlot mingled. She allowed her hands to inch under his shirt and to caress the warm, taut skin beneath it.

Mason moaned and broke off the kiss, but only to trail his mouth eagerly over her cheek and down her neck.

"Yes," she murmured and he echoed the sentiment.

His warm breath made her shiver in anticipation, or maybe it was his hands and the way they had pulled up her top and brushed against her bare midriff in a caress that left her skin feeling singed. He did not resemble a patient man now, and it secretly delighted Roz that she could push him to the brink of insanity, for she didn't doubt for a moment that what was happening between them was insane.

I must be out of my mind, Mason thought. He hadn't intended this scene when he'd asked Rose to come inside. He could admit he'd been fantasizing about getting her into his bed quite often lately, but when it happened—*if* it happened—he'd planned to keep the pace slow.

His body didn't seem to care about his plans, though. He pulled back, tried to regain his balance. Rose just stared at him, her eyes large and watchful. He lifted a hand to her hair, running his fingers through the short, spiky mess that had captivated him from the first.

"It used to be long," she said quietly.

He tried to picture it, to picture anything but the erotic scene that was already playing in his mind. He cleared his throat. "How long?"

She held an index finger to the middle of her upper arm. "It was…pretty."

"It's pretty now."

She offered a lopsided grin that squeezed his heart. "No, it's easy now."

"Okay, but I like it."

"Really?"

"Really," he replied. "It's very Meg Ryan-ish. And I've always had this thing for Meg Ryan."

He settled his lips over hers. Where he had allowed her to initiate and set the pace for the last kiss, he decided to call all of the shots this time. Words could only convey so much. He used his hands and mouth to express his feelings, to tell her she was beautiful, desirable, wanted.

She moaned when he nipped her earlobe, sighed when he caressed the slope of one cheek, shivered when his fingers glided up her spine. He'd never met a woman so re-

sponsive to simple touches, simple plea-
sures. It fueled his imagination and his own
need.

"Do you like this?" he asked, bringing
his fingers around to trail up her torso. He
stopped just below the curve of one small,
perfect breast and waited as she sucked in
a breath and managed a shaky nod.

"Stay with me," he murmured, nuzzling
her neck.

Rose never got a chance to answer. The
door banged opened and Marnie breezed
in.

"Anybody home?" his sister called as
she rounded the corner into the kitchen.

Mason yanked his hand out from beneath
Rose's shirt with a guilty start.

"Oh, my," was all Marnie said.

Rose tried to step away, but Mason
stopped her. He kept her in the circle of his
arms, even as he felt his face heat to the
same color as the marinara. He didn't need
to look at Marnie's cat-that-swallowed-the-
canary grin to know she was enjoying this.

"Looks like I interrupted something,"
she said. Her amused gaze dipped to the
half-empty wineglasses and the discarded

sweaters heaped on the floor before returning to Mason's face.

"Yeah, and maybe next time you'll think to call first," he said irritably.

His brother-in-law, God bless him, came in then.

"Oh, gosh, Mason. Sorry. Come on, Marnie. We'll just come back another time."

He backed toward the door, but Marnie grabbed Hal's hand and pulled him fully into the kitchen.

"We're here and the moment has been ruined. Right, Mason?" She smiled wickedly. "We might as well stay and tell them why we came."

Mason sighed heavily and prayed for patience.

"Can't you do something about her?" he asked Hal.

Hal just shook his head, but he was smiling, too, when he replied, "You know your sister."

Indeed he did. And he planned to make her pay for this. But she was right. The moment was ruined. Blown to bits, even if his ardor hadn't quite cooled. In fact, he had little doubt that if he stepped away from Rose right now, his body's very aroused state would be impossible for his uninvited guests to miss. And Mason knew Marnie would take great delight in teasing him about it. The woman had no shame.

"Would you at least give us a minute and go wait in the living room," he said from between gritted teeth.

At least in this, Marnie complied. When they were alone in the kitchen, Mason dropped a kiss on Rose's forehead and sighed heavily.

"Sorry about this."

"Your sister has lousy timing," she said.

"Maybe it was for the best," Mason replied. "We kind of lost our heads."

"Actually I think it was our shirts that we lost," she teased, bending down to scoop up the sweaters. She handed one to him and pulled on her own.

"Are you regretting it?" he asked.

"Not exactly. You?"

"Not exactly."

"But you're thinking it's not smart. This…" She wiggled a hand between the two of them.

"Probably not. I really like you, Rose."

She smiled up at him, but he'd never seen her look quite so vulnerable.

"There's a 'but' coming, isn't there?"

"Afraid so. I'm really attracted to you. It would be stupid to deny it given what has already happened between us. But there's a lot of...unsettled business in your life right now. I don't want to take advantage of you or the situation."

"I see."

"I just think that this..." He motioned with his hand, not knowing exactly how to define the *this* to which he obliquely referred. "This wouldn't be a good situation for either one of us if...you'll be leaving."

"That's been my plan all along," she agreed.

Was it still? She waited for him to ask her, but he didn't. And she didn't know what her answer would have been anyway.

"I'm making a mess of this, aren't I? I'm just trying to be a gentleman."

And he was being a gentleman, a perfect gentleman. But Roz still felt hurt, rejected. And the swift, sharp pain of it surprised her. After being abandoned by her biological mother, dismissed from foster families and tossed aside by the state when she reached her majority, what could anyone else do to hurt her? But her heart, battered as it was, had never been broken by a man. Now it seemed perilously close to shattering.

"Just for the record, I don't hop into bed casually, no matter what it might have seemed like a few minutes ago."

"I know that, Rose. And the same goes for me. Neither one of us is the casual sort, which is why I think we need to step back from this, gain some perspective."

"Perspective." She said the word slowly, idly wondering how it would be spelled. P-U-R...P-E-R...

"It means—"

"I know what it means, Mason," she said sharply.

His attempt to educate her highlighted the wide gulf between their lives. A man like Mason had never given her a second glance before. And she was sure Mason had never been interested in someone like her, a semiliterate nobody who didn't even know her real name or date of birth. Maybe that was the perspective he was talking about.

She picked up her wine and tossed it

back in a single swallow, wishing it was something much stronger. Fermented grape juice wasn't enough to anesthetize this sudden, searing pain. Holding the thin stem between her fingers, she pretended to inspect the now-empty goblet.

"It's a pity you wasted all this wine on someone like me."

"Why would you say that, Rose?"

She shrugged. "Just out of curiosity, how long has it been since you had a...a physical relationship?"

"What has sex got to do—?"

"How long?" she asked again.

"A year."

"Ah. The woman you took a bullet for. No wonder you're gun-shy. No pun intended." She wasn't being fair, but then self-preservation rarely was. "Still, that's a long time to go without sex. I guess I can understand why you found me so tempting."

"That's not the case and you know it." Real anger sparked in his usually calm eyes. "Abstinence isn't the issue here. What's happening between us goes well beyond hormones."

He looked surprised after he said it. And not particularly happy.

"Mason, Rose, are you coming?" Marnie called from the other room.

Mason closed his eyes and Roz got the feeling he was praying for patience. She knew she was on the verge of losing her cool as well.

"Let's go find out what Marnie is dying to tell us," she said.

"This isn't over, not by a long shot."

Old survival instincts kicked in. Reject before being rejected. "There is no *this*, Mason."

Of course, they both knew that was a lie.

Mason stood in the kitchen and took a few moments to regroup mentally before he followed her into the living room. He'd hurt Rose's feelings with his clumsy words; he knew that now. And he also realized that the heart he was trying to protect with his determination to step back and gain perspective wasn't Rose's.

It was his own.

Marnie and Hal were seated on the couch. Rose stood looking out one of the tall, thin windows that faced the lake when he joined them.

"So, what's so important that you felt the need to barge into my home on a Sunday afternoon?" he said when he walked into the room.

Marnie flashed a dazzling grin, a twin to the one on her husband's face.

"We're having a baby!"

Marnie kissed her husband after she said it, and then jumped up to give Mason a hug.

"We wanted you to be the first to know."

"Aw, Marnie." He hugged her hard, kissed her cheek and said, "Don't think this gets you off the hook. You're still going to pay for barging in without calling or at least knocking first."

"I love you, too," she replied.

Roz watched the scene with wonder, processing the pure joy on Marnie's face, the excitement on Hal's and the happiness on Mason's. A child would be coming into the world, welcomed into this family. It was already loved, already cherished. This was how it was supposed to be, she knew. Still, it seemed almost too good to be true.

Her resolve hardened. She wanted to find her mother. She needed to confront the woman who'd given birth to her and then abandoned her. She needed answers.

What makes me so unwanted, so unlovable? What makes me so dispensable and disposable?

She crossed the room to Marnie and let the other woman enfold her in a hug as Mason and Hal were shaking hands and slapping backs.

"Congratulations. I'm happy for you."

"And I'm happy for you," Marnie replied meaningfully.

"It wasn't…we're not…we just got carried away by the moment."

Mischief danced in Marnie's gaze and she patted her still flat stomach. "So did Hal and I."

Later that night, Mason walked along the shoreline. The moon was nearly full in a cloudless sky and it illuminated the ice that was buckled and piled high on the beach not far from the lighthouse. He felt restless and unsettled as he turned the afternoon's events over in his mind. He hadn't meant to hurt Rose's feelings, and he was sure he had, no matter what she claimed. She thought she was so tough, so thick-skinned, but her vulnerability had always been apparent to him. Maybe that was what drew him to her.

He rubbed his shoulder, the ache serving as a reminder of what had happened the last time Mason had felt this tangled up over a woman in need. He'd lost all perspective, rushed in with his heart and almost paid with his life.

And the woman he'd loved? He stopped, kicked at the ice with the tip of one of his heavy boots. She'd bluffed her way through rehab, gotten herself a new, more discreet dealer, and never returned Mason's phone calls. He'd no longer been necessary once her daddy knew all about the extent of their relationship. Amelia had lived for the thrill. And the thrill was gone as far as she was concerned.

But Mason had still cared enough about her to bring her continued drug dependence to the senator's attention. He'd expected shock, outrage. And those emotions had been there, but only because Bertrand hadn't wanted Mason on the case any longer, digging into the family's business.

Apparently Amelia's dependency on cocaine was okay since she bought it from some white-collared dealer rather than the crack she'd purchased from shady, violent characters in the inner-city.

Mason had felt sucker-punched. He'd believed in Senator Bertrand, so much so he had campaigned for him in the previous election. Now he knew the senator was a liar and a fraud. His anti-drug crusade was just a gimmick. It played well, especially with middle-class voters living the American dream in suburbia. But in reality, he didn't care about dealers or even those poor souls who found themselves sucked into using. Even his own daughter's addiction was of no consequence, as long as it was kept quiet.

Of course, the good Senator Bertrand had compensated Mason well. He'd paid all of his hospital bills and sent him a nice, fat check. The money said, "Go away and be quiet." Mason had been too disillusioned to do otherwise. He'd come back to Chance Harbor and any thought he'd entertained about politics had withered. As for women, he'd easily steered clear of them.

He watched the beacon sweep the frozen harbor.

Until Rose.

February ebbed into March, leaving tiny Chance Harbor frosted with a blanket of white. If spring were just around the corner, one wouldn't know it from the frigid temperatures and the continual snowfall.

Roz had already managed to save a hundred dollars after paying rent and buying Marnie a thank-you gift for all the clothes and household items she'd so kindly donated to Roz's cause. In the weeks Roz had been in Chance Harbor, she and Marnie had become fast friends.

That was a real first. Roz had made many male friends over the years. Perhaps her tomboy demeanor had something to do with that. Or, perhaps it was that she felt more at ease around guys—most guys, she amended, thinking of Mason. But she found it easy to talk and share confidences with Marnie. Except when it came to Mason. Roz never mentioned him and she feigned indifference whenever Marnie brought him up.

She did so now as the other woman all but cornered her behind the bar.

"What is with my brother lately? He's so...I don't know, just not himself. Very distracted. He's gotten three of my drink orders wrong in the past couple of hours. Did you two have a fight or something?"

"A fight? What would we fight over?"

Marnie put her hands on her hips and raised her eyebrows knowingly. "Honey, men and women have been finding things to fight over since Adam and Eve and that unfortunate apple incident."

Bergen dinged the order bell, saving Roz from having to continue this uncomfortable conversation.

Or so she thought. But when she returned from delivering dinner to two state troopers, Marnie was not giving up. She sat at the bar, studying her brother over a tall glass of iced tea. Mason was playing pool with Hal. He glanced their way—and scratched.

"Well, something's bothering him." She slanted a look at Roz. "Or someone."

Roz picked up a damp rag and wiped down the bar, even though she had already done so twice.

"I don't know what you mean."

"Oh, come on. You two were wrapped around each other like a pair of vines that day in his kitchen and now he's all crabby and distracted. The last time Mason was this tightly wound, he ended up being..."

Marnie stopped, blushed.

"Shot."

"I was going to say, in love," Marnie said primly.

"Somehow I don't think Mason draws a distinction between the two. What was she like?"

"Who?"

"The woman in Detroit."

"Amelia Bertrand?"

Was she pretty, Roz wondered?

And then realized she'd spoken the question aloud when Marnie replied, "From the pictures I've seen of her, yes. Her father is a U.S. senator. Very much the big shot. He heads up appropriations."

So, this was the important someone who had hired Mason to keep his daughter out of trouble.

Marnie was saying, "She helps her father campaign, even when he's giving speeches about the scourge of illegal drugs and how the penalties should be stiffer for users as well as dealers.''

Mason's aversion to politics was starting to make sense.

''It's pathetic,'' Marnie said, shaking her head. ''But she's attractive enough that I'm sure she pulls in a lot of the male vote. She sure had Mason fooled.''

It was hard to picture Mason trailing after some female with adoration blurring his vision, especially since the woman in question was also an assignment. Roz experienced a kick of jealousy, which she immediately dismissed as mere envy. And somehow the distinction seemed more acceptable. After all, no one had ever looked at her that way. It really wasn't about Mason, she told herself. Just the emotion.

''What color hair does she have? Is she tall?''

''Why does it matter?''

It didn't, but it did. It *really* did.

Still, Roz shrugged nonchalantly. ''Just trying to figure out if I've seen the commercials she's been in with her father.''

''Not quite as tall as you,'' Marnie replied, giving Roz the once-over. ''I'd say five-six. As for hair, blond, a couple shades lighter than yours.''

Roz did sigh this time. ''Long, right? Past her shoulders?''

''Yeah. Have you seen her?''

''No.''

''Then how'd you know?''

''Because God has a well-honed sense of irony,'' Roz murmured, fingertips playing with the ends of her butchered locks and remembering how they had once trailed to the middle of her back.

CHAPTER SEVEN

Two weeks passed. Two long weeks during which Roz carefully avoided being alone with Mason. And he made it easy. They no longer skied in the mornings. The first week after getting carried away in his kitchen, they both had found excuses not to and then the weather cooperated with a warming spell that made the trails too slushy to navigate.

But as Roz walked into the tavern just before her shift this evening, Mason not only looked up from his usual place behind the bar, he waved her over.

As she walked toward him, he grinned and Roz felt her traitorous pulse pick up speed. God, did the man have to be that gorgeous?

''What's up?'' she asked nonchalantly when she reached him.

''I think I've got a lead.''

She frowned. ''A lead?''

"On your mother. You're still interested in finding her, right?"

She gave a jerky nod, unable to identify all of the messy emotions suddenly sloshing through her. Of all the things she had expected him to say to her, this was nowhere on the list. She felt blindsided, both by the fact he might have found a starting point to unraveling her past and because he was searching in the first place. She'd just assumed, given the strain between the two of them, that he wasn't on the case.

"You've been looking?"

"I said I would."

"But that was…" She glanced around and even though no one sat close enough to hear her, she lowered her voice. "Before."

"I keep my promises, Rose. Come on back to the office so we can talk in private."

She followed him, feeling a little dazed. And, though she didn't want to admit it, excited. The moment the office door closed behind them, she asked, "So, what's the lead?"

Mason walked behind his desk and rifled through some papers.

"I've been contacting old friends from the Detroit police force and some of the folks I knew at the Family Independence Agency," he said, referring to the state agency that oversaw the foster care system.

Roz took a deep breath and let it out slowly.

Don't get your hopes up, she told herself. But her heart was hammering as if she'd just run a marathon. She didn't want to be this excited. Apathy had been her shield for so long. Now, she felt exposed, vulnerable in a way she'd long told herself she wouldn't allow.

"I had a friend at the department look up the report from the day you were found. A woman who lived nearby had called the police when she spotted you. I've got her name, number. If she's still in the area maybe she'll be willing to tell me something she wouldn't tell the police."

"Oh."

"It's a long shot," Mason admitted. "But I've just gotten started."

He stepped around the desk and gave her arm a squeeze.

"We'll find her, Rose."

She crossed her arms, feeling warmed by his touch and oddly chilled at the same time. Too much was happening inside her head, thoughts and feelings she couldn't process and didn't understand. And the man standing in front of her played a big part in the muddle.

"Are you okay?" he asked.

"Sure." She shrugged. "I keep telling myself not to think about finding my mother, but it's pretty much all I've been thinking about lately," she admitted.

It had crowded her thoughts, eased into her dreams. Right along with Mason.

"All?" he asked with a lift of one brow.

"What else would I be thinking about?" she challenged.

He glanced away and she didn't think he would answer. But then his gaze cut back to hers and she saw something in his eyes that made her suck in a breath.

"Same thing I've been thinking about. You do things to me, Rose," he said on a sigh and rubbed a hand over his face. "I'm not sure I like feeling this way."

"What way is that?" But she hoped she knew.

"Like I'm going to go crazy if I don't have you."

Oh, yeah. They were on the same page there.

"Well, you said we should step back. Something about gaining perspective," she reminded him.

He closed his eyes. "Yeah, I said that."

And despite his grimace, she was determined not to cut him any slack.

"You said you didn't want to take advantage of my—what did you call it?—ah, yes, *situation.*"

One eye opened. "Uh-huh."

"Something about me having a lot of baggage."

Both eyes were open now. "I never said baggage."

"What then?"

"I think I called it *unsettled business.*" He stared at her mouth as he said it.

"Is there a difference?"

"Uh-huh."

Mason took a step toward her until he stood so close she could feel his warm breath caress against her cheek as he repeated, "Unsettled business."

The kiss that followed was far from gentle. It was a mating of mouths, a hot, fervent welcoming and acknowledgment of need. Roz's fingers fisted tightly into the soft material of Mason's chambray shirt until she thought the fabric might rend. She felt his hands slide lower until they rested on her bottom.

She'd missed those hands.

"I've had dreams about picking up where we left off that day in my kitchen," he said.

"That makes two of us," she felt brave enough to admit.

She spied the clock on the far wall. She had a couple minutes before her shift started and she planned to make the most of them. Her fingers traveled to the buttons running down the front of Mason's shirt. She'd just fished the first one through its hole when the door opened and Bergen walked in.

"Oh, jeez!" the cook exclaimed in a voice reminiscent of Archie Bunker's.

Mason, usually so calm and unflappable, swore lavishly. And Roz agreed completely with the stark sentiment.

"Doesn't anybody knock anymore?"

The crusty cook wasn't put off by his boss's show of temper.

"She gonna start work at some point today, or is this where she'll be earning her paycheck?"

"Watch your mouth, Bergen." The words were said in a low pitch that made them all the more menacing.

"So, that's the way it is between you and Roz?" Bergen asked. And it dawned on Roz that he was the only person in Chance Harbor who didn't call her Rose.

"That's the way it is," Mason confirmed. "That's *exactly* the way it is."

For the first time in her life, Roz realized she had a champion. For the first time in her life, somebody wanted her. And she believed Mason when he said it was about more than sex. Maybe someday, he could love her, too.

Because the thought left her feeling unsteady and as if she might break down and blubber, she gave Mason a quick peck on the cheek and then stepped away from him.

"I'd better get to work." She brushed past Bergen, but then paused at the door to look back at Mason. "I really appreciate your help with the...um, family thing."

"We'll find her," he said.

Roz nodded. For now, at least, it was enough that he was looking.

Bergen wanted to pick a fight. He made it clear during the rest of the evening. Whenever Roz came within earshot, he offered some insulting comment or another. She didn't say a word in return. She had met lots of Bergens in her life—people who never looked past her rough edges. She wouldn't waste her time trying to win him over. Such an effort would be frustrating and ultimately futile. She decided she would just ignore him.

But her plan went up in smoke when she found herself in his company after closing time. Mason was in his office finishing up preparations for the tavern's annual St.

Patrick's Day party. And the other waitress had clocked out early that night because of a family emergency.

She took a deep breath and walked into the kitchen with the mop and pail. She barely had a chance to wring out the excess water and slap the mop head down on the floor before Bergen started in on her.

"Think you've got a pretty slick setup here, don't you? You've got the boss all twisted into knots. The man can't keep his hands off you even in a place of business. It's sick, that's what it is."

She stopped mopping and leaned against the handle. "Don't go there," she warned softly.

"Nice little scene I interrupted between the pair of you earlier. What are you hoping to get in return for your *services,* besides reading lessons?"

"Leave Mason out of this, Bergen. You don't like me, fine. It's mutual, believe me. I know I'm no beauty queen. I know I'm no Rhodes scholar. I've never been much of anything, truth be told. But I'm no whore. Mason is…Mason is…"

She swallowed thickly, mortified by the tears that clogged her throat.

"Mason is out of your league, girlie," he finished for her. "When you leaving?"

"I might not be going," she challenged, lifting her chin.

But all of that wonderful new confidence she'd felt earlier in the day wilted like the old lettuce leaves Bergen had tossed in the garbage.

"My cousin is selling his car. It's not much to look at, but it runs good. He's asking nine hundred, but I can get him down some. I'll even kick in a couple hundred bucks."

"Why would you do that?"

"Ain't 'cause I like you. I'd do it 'cause I want you gone. And because Mason's daddy gave me this job and I promised him and Mrs. Striker I'd keep an eye on the boy when they retired to Arizona."

"Your generosity is overwhelming."

"What do you say?"

Oh, she had plenty to say, but she swallowed the pithy response and instead replied, "I've got work to do."

*　　*　　*

It was after three o'clock in the morning when Roz finally collapsed onto her bed. Despite being bone-tired, sleep eluded her.

She thought about the kiss she and Mason had shared in his office. Like his previous kisses, it left her keyed up and wanting more. Wanting too much. But the question that grated on her was, what did Mason want? *Really* want. As much as she longed to ask, she was afraid of what his answer would be.

The sex would be great. A man that patient and thorough would no doubt leave a woman satisfied. Limited though her experience might be, Roz knew passion only took a relationship so far. And it would burn out eventually without something more meaningful to fuel it.

Love.

Once upon a time, Roz had worried she wasn't capable of that complex emotion. Maybe she wasn't wired for long-term commitments given her history. How could she be when every person of importance in her life had merely passed through it?

But the emotion she was feeling—as alien and terrifying as it was—was definitely love. Fragile, yet she knew it would not be fleeting.

When are you leaving? Bergen had asked. For the first time in her life, Roz didn't know the answer. It wasn't because she didn't want to stay. She did. But it wasn't enough for her to want to remain, she realized. Someone had to want her here as well. Mason.

The Lighthouse Tavern was the pub of choice on St. Patrick's Day. Every seat was occupied. Boisterous revelers bellied up to every inch of bar space. The beer flowed as green and as generous as the tip money, and Roz swore more people in Chance Harbor claimed to be Irish than lived in all of Dublin.

After the lunch crowd left, Mason and Bergen moved the pool table out to make room for a band that had been booked for the evening. To Roz's amazement and amusement, it wasn't a head-banging band but one that specialized in Irish ballads and jigs.

The singer, a clean-cut man who spoke with a slight brogue, was at the mike now leading the crowd in a rousing rendition of "Little Brown Jug."

Mason had told her that the guy taught high school in the next county over, but he could trace his family's roots to the Emerald Isle and, later, New York.

Roz delivered another pitcher of green beer and pocketed the sizable tip. If this kept up she'd have enough money to buy one of those interesting little nighties she'd seen in the Victoria's Secret catalog. She smiled at the fantasy that came to mind.

"That smile for me, sugar?" Brice Battle asked. He caught her off guard, which was why he managed to plop her down in his lap with a quick tug on her arm.

The old Roz would have decked him before bolting for the exit. This Roz was more refined. She discreetly jabbed a sharp elbow into his paunch as she regained her feet and then offered a superior smile. "The only thing I have for you, *sugar,* is the check."

"Saving it all for Mason, eh?" He reached for her hand again, but she neatly dodged him this time. "Come on, he won't mind sharing."

"I'd mind," Mason said. He stood behind Roz, so close in fact that she swore she could feel the heat from his body. It was tempting to lean back into all of that warmth. But this was a place of business—*Mason's* place of business. She wouldn't embarrass him in that way. No one in town, except Bergen and Marnie, knew for certain if there was anything between the two of them other than a W-4 form and rent money.

But Mason cleared that up when he said in a voice loud enough to compete with the band, "Keep your hands off my woman."

And then, with half of the bar looking on, he kissed Roz full on the mouth.

Even before the kiss ended, the band's lead singer was at the microphone saying, "We've got a request for 'My Love is Like a Red, Red Rose.' We'll try to do it justice." As the music began, the singer added, "This one is dedicated to Mason."

Mason glanced up, surprised.

"Thought you might like to ask Rose to

dance,'' Marnie said from behind him. "I'll cover the bar."

"Sometimes you're all right, sis,'' he told her and then led Roz to the small dance floor.

It was crowded with couples already, but Roz still felt conspicuous. Even so, when Mason held out his hand to her, she went into his arms and tried to follow his steps.

Two forward, one back. They'd done this once before, but it all seemed so new this time and so awkward now that they had an audience.

"You're doing good," Mason whispered in her ear. "I can hardly tell you're counting."

She flashed a rueful grin. "Thanks."

"And you look beautiful, by the way. Did you do something different with your hair?"

"Combed it." She laughed and resisted the urge to fiddle with the ends that she had blow-dried like Marnie suggested so that they curled up in the back and at the nape. She'd even applied a little gel to hold it in place. "Actually it's due for a cut, but I'm thinking about growing it out."

"Short or long, I have a feeling you'll still be driving me crazy."

The song's tempo was slow, the lyrics lovely and the singer's sweet tenor more than did justice to the words.

"This is a pretty song," she said.

"Actually, it was first a poem, 'A Red, Red Rose' by Robert Burns." And he surprised her by singing along: "'As fair art thou, my bonnie lass/ So deep in love am I/ And I will love thee still, my dear/ Till all the seas gang dry.'"

She swallowed, touched by the words and not at all embarrassed to ask, "Gang dry?"

"It means go."

She shook her head in amazement. He'd been a cop and a private investigator, and had been shot for his trouble. And yet he also knew about birds and tree bark, how to slow dance, sing and even interpret the lines of a poem penned by some long-dead white guy.

"How do you know all this stuff?" she asked.

"Books," Mason shrugged. "I'll check out a collection of Burns' poetry from the library." He wiggled his eyebrows. "I hear it can really set the mood."

Roz thought back to the lingerie she'd been considering splurging on.

"I know something else that can set the mood, too."

"Oh?" His eyes went smoky and she knew she had his full attention.

"Something small, silky. It covers just enough to keep a man curious."

"Good thing I used to be a private investigator. I have an insatiable...curiosity. Maybe we should plan a date."

"A date?"

"Ever been on one?" he asked.

There was no laughter in his gaze or in his tone. And so it shamed Roz only a little to admit, "No, never."

"Then I'll look forward to being your first."

And she wished he could have been the first in that other important way. The memory of her first sexual encounter hadn't improved with age. There was nothing about the quick and painful coupling with a boy she'd met in high school detention to romanticize. She could admit now that the need to be touched had held more importance at the time than seeking any kind of release. It hadn't satisfied her that way, let alone in any other.

"Mason, I'm not a v—"

He cut off her words with a kiss.

"I know, Rose. Me, either. But it'll be special with you."

The song ended and the band's leader began to sing a poignant song about young Willie McBride who died at age nineteen during the First World War. Roz told herself that was why her eyes began to well with tears. Damn song. The Irish really knew how to tug at one's heart.

And so did Mason.

Nearly an hour after closing time the band wound up its last set with "Danny Boy," leaving not a dry eye in the place. When the musicians had packed up their mandolins, guitars, banjos, drums and pennywhistles and collected their fee, most of the bar patrons left with them, the overimbibed ones among them being poured into the cars of sober friends and relatives.

It was well after four when the last of

the spilt green beer had been mopped up and peanut shells swept away.

From the neatly stocked shelf behind the bar Mason selected a bottle of whiskey.

"Want a little bit of the Irish?" he asked Rose, pouring two fingers into a glass for himself.

She mustered up a slight smile and set the mop aside. "If you'd offered me a green beer, I would have had to hurt you."

She jingled when she walked across the room to him, pockets bulging with the fruits of her labor.

"Tips good tonight?"

"Very." She grinned.

"Know any Irish toasts?" Mason asked.

"One. I learned it from foster mom number four. The family was Irish." She cleared her throat. *"There are good ships and there are wood ships, the ships that sail the sea. But the best ships are friend-ships and may that always be."*

"Slainte," Mason said and took a healthy sip.

Rose gave him a wicked wink and tossed back the contents of her glass in a single gulp that inspired neither a coughing fit nor watering eyes. She returned the empty glass to the bar with a click.

Only Rose could make such a gesture seem sexy, he thought.

"Ready to go?" she asked.

"Let me just lock up."

A few minutes later they walked out into the quiet night. The air was crisp, but Mason welcomed it. Anything to cool down the blood pooling low in his body. He reached for her hand as they walked toward the lighthouse. He'd left his Jeep parked at home that day.

"So, are you free this Saturday night?"

"I'll have to check with my boss," she replied coyly.

"You're free."

"Paid night off?" she asked.

"Don't push it."

"Where do you plan to take me?"

He hadn't really thought about it.

"How about Paradise?"

"You aim high," she said.

"Not really. It's a little town over on Whitefish Bay."

He chuckled after he said it and Rose slugged him in the arm.

"I'll take that as a no." As they walked up the winding gravel driveway to the lighthouse, he asked, "How about New York?"

"Sure. You're paying my airfare, right?" She laughed, but Mason stopped walking.

"Yes."

She swung around and even in the darkness Mason could tell she was surprised.

"Are you serious?"

"Uh-huh. Ever been?"

"To New York? No. I was heading west when we met, remember?" She said it lightly, but was not quite successful at hiding the fact that she was good and flustered.

And Mason was glad.

"It's been a while since I've been there, but I've been meaning to go back. I think you'll like it. There's something for everyone in New York. Not to mention some of the best food anywhere on the planet."

"You want to take me to New York for dinner?"

"I'll throw in a Broadway show, too."

"New York," she repeated inanely.

"Yes." He reached for her hand and

tugged her close. "We can fly out of the little airport in Houghton early Saturday to Detroit, catch a connection and be in New York before the afternoon. Then we can come back either late Sunday or even Monday morning if you'd like. I want to be alone with you, Rose."

"We don't have to go to New York to be alone. Bolt the door so Marnie doesn't barge in and I'll settle for beer and pizza at your place."

He knew she would and that's why it seemed so important suddenly to take her someplace exciting, special.

"New York. What do you say?"

She didn't reply. She kissed him instead. Even with her cold fingers brushing his back where she'd untucked his shirt, Mason felt ready to go up in flames. God, the woman did things to him.

When they reached the garage, he stood at the base of the steps and watched till she had opened the apartment door at the top.

"I can't wait till Saturday," she called to him before slipping inside.

Mason sucked in a deep breath of frigid air, hoping to cool off.

Neither can I, he thought. Neither can I.

CHAPTER EIGHT

THE weather was nice enough on Friday morning that Mason decided to go for a jog. He logged five miles along the highway that ran parallel to Superior's shore and he was feeling pretty smug about the fact he had managed to keep his mind off Rose—and what the pair of them hopefully would be doing together the following night.

When he reached the lighthouse driveway, he slowed to a walk. Then, when he was nearly to the side door, he bent at the waist and waited for his breathing to even out. He spied the package as he straightened, and his settled pulse kicked higher than the hooves of a rodeo bull.

Victoria's Secret, the return address said. Every man's fantasy was stowed in that innocuous-looking parcel. Imagination was both blessing and curse, he decided, stifling a groan as his already overworked libido took off again.

Then a thought came to him that had his blood running cold and ardor cooling fast. His sister was known to use his address for deliveries when she wanted to surprise her husband.

Please, God, don't let this be for Marnie.

It took him a moment to work up the courage to look a little lower on the label.

Miss Rosalind Bennett.

"Thank you!" he said aloud.

He carried the package inside and dropped it onto the counter in the kitchen. Then he stripped off the sweatshirt he wore over a stained gray Detroit Police Department T-shirt, mopped his face with it and grabbed a carton of orange juice out of the fridge. Taking a swig from the spout, he contemplated the box.

What had Rose ordered? And what would she look like wearing it?

He picked up the package and shook it, and then felt like a child caught snooping under the tree before Christmas when a knock sounded on his back door and he heard Rose call out, "It's just me."

No *just* about it, he thought, as he hollered back, "Come on in." And then he took another gulp of juice.

When Rose walked into the kitchen, his breath stuttered in his chest. She was wearing makeup, just enough to make her eyelashes look heavier, longer and somewhat exotic. And her hair was a good two shades lighter than it used to be.

"Y-you look different," he said.

"Marnie's doing," she replied with a wave of her hand. "She came over this morning and did the whole beauty-shop thing on me. Said something about it being essential since I would have a chance to visit the holy trinity while I was in New York."

"Huh?"

"Saks Fifth Avenue, Neiman-Marcus and Bergdorf's." Rose angled her head to one side. "Your sister's weird."

"Yeah, but she does have good taste. You look nice. And I like the hair."

"Me, too. I guess it was worth having her shove a plastic cap on my head and then pull strands of my hair through a bunch of little holes with what looked like a crochet hook."

Mason didn't have a clue what she was

talking about, but it sounded like torture. Still, he liked the results. He *really* liked the results.

"What's that you've got in your hand?" she asked.

He glanced down and felt his face heat.

"Oh, this came for you." He thrust the package toward her. "I found it outside my door when I got back from my run. I was just going to bring it up."

A smile bloomed on her lips, which he realized were glossed to the color of ripe strawberries and entirely too inviting.

She made a satisfied little humming sound in the back of her throat before saying, "I was really hoping this was going to arrive today."

Which, to Mason's way of thinking, meant she planned to bring whatever Victoria had sent with her to New York. A chorus of *Hallelujah* rang in his head.

He plucked the juice back off the counter and gestured toward the package with it. "You going to open it?"

"Right now?"

"Why not?" he replied, with a casual lift of his shoulders.

"Nah. Not yet. I want these to be a surprise."

The juice carton stopped midway to his lips.

"These?" He swallowed thickly.

What exactly were *these*? Mason wanted to know, but he didn't ask, because the odds were good that something in that package would send a grown man to his knees begging.

"Just some...stuff."

"Lacy stuff?"

"Might be."

Roz offered a slow smile so full of promise he was forced to press his lips together to keep his tongue from lolling out. And, at that moment, he understood perfectly why Adam had taken a bite of the apple, why war had been waged over Helen, and why a throne had been abdicated over the divorcée Simpson.

"Mason?"

Rose stepped forward, leaving their faces mere inches apart. He could smell the clean scent of her—soap and shampoo and minty toothpaste when she breathed out his name.

"Yes?"

"Tomorrow night you're going to find

out firsthand why they call New York the city that never sleeps.''

He couldn't think of a thing to say in response. His tongue felt glued to the roof of his mouth. And his fingers felt as if they'd lost all feeling, which is why, he supposed, the juice carton slid free and its contents splattered all over the floor.

Despite her brazen words the day before in Mason's kitchen, when their plane landed at New York's LaGuardia Airport, Roz's bravado failed her. The nearer the yellow cab driven by a man with a death wish brought them to their midtown Manhattan hotel, the more nervous Roz became.

What if after she and Mason went a few rounds between the sheets and satisfied their mutual need and curiosity he realized there was really nothing else between them? What if he finally realized she was nothing special, nothing worth the time, effort and now money he'd spent on her?

Oh, he would be kind when he broke the news to her. Roz didn't doubt that. It wasn't in his nature to be cruel. But some wounds cut to the bone regardless of how delicately the blow was delivered.

"You're quiet." Mason reached over and gave her hand a squeeze.

"This makes Detroit seem small-town," she replied, hoping he would accept that as an excuse for her laconic behavior.

"And Chance Harbor seem positively minuscule," he added.

"Do you ever miss living in the city?"

"At times. But Chance Harbor will always be home. What about you?"

City, country, Roz had never had a preference. Just as she'd never had a home. Not a real one like the kind Mason spoke of with such casual fondness. But she shrugged and said, "Sure, sometimes. There's a lot to do in the city, especially at night."

"Waldorf-Astoria," the cabdriver said, as the vehicle lurched to a stop outside the distinctive entrance of the hotel.

Roz sucked in a breath and then let it out slowly between her teeth. "We're here," she said brightly.

But when she reached for the door handle, Mason stopped her.

"Are you nervous, Rose?"

"Why would I be nervous?" She

worked up a grin. "I have stayed in a hotel a time or two before."

"That's not what I meant. We don't have to...we can get separate rooms, you know."

It was just about the sweetest thing a man had ever said to her. And it helped to quell her nerves enough that the next smile she offered felt less brittle.

"Getting cold feet?"

His expression was dead serious when he replied: "Nothing about me has had a chance to cool down in quite some time where you're concerned. But I don't want you to feel pressured."

She leaned over, kissed him lightly on the lips.

"I don't."

Roz hadn't lied when she'd told Mason she'd stayed in a hotel a time or two, but nothing about those fleabag establishments could compare to the Waldorf-Astoria. After checking in, Mason had the bellman carry their bags upstairs and they walked around the lower level. He'd stayed there once before, and so he gave her a guided tour, stopping at the round mosaic on the floor of the Park Avenue lobby, before moving on to the central lobby, with its nine-foot-tall clock.

On the way to the elevators, Roz stopped beside a massive fresh floral arrangement that scented the air with lilies.

"It's beautiful," she said, and then turned in a semicircle. "All of it is, Mason. I didn't expect…this."

"I go all out when I'm trying to impress a woman," he replied. "This place is an Art Deco landmark."

"I don't know Art Deco from Etch A Sketch, but thank you. I'll never forget this, Mason. Any of it."

"Then I'll just have to make sure it's all worth remembering."

They took the elevator to their room. Or, rather, their suite. A fire burned cheerfully in the hearth and despite the early hour, champagne was already chilling in a silver bucket atop the wet bar. French doors separated the living room from the bedroom. They had been left open. Inside, at the foot of a king-sized bed, she spied the suitcase Marnie had lent her standing next to the one Mason had brought.

No one had ever treated her to such luxury. She'd never mattered enough for anyone to try to impress her. She felt the first tears threaten, stinging her eyes, making her throat ache. Ridiculous, she thought, to want to cry when someone was trying to make her happy.

"There's a great view of Park Avenue," Mason said when she hadn't moved from her spot just inside the door.

She walked to where he stood holding back the curtain. Several stories below, the traffic buzzed along, and she could hear the faint blare of horns and the hum of revving engines through the glass.

Mason let the curtain fall back and then pulled her into his arms.

"I don't know why or how, but I think I've made you sad."

"No, not sad. Overwhelmed. You make me feel special, Mason, and I've never felt that way before."

She stood on tiptoe, started to kiss him, but he pulled back.

"Let's get one thing straight. I don't want gratitude. That's not what this is all about. I treat you special because you are."

When she only smiled, he gave her a little shake. "You are, Rose."

"How special?" she asked on a broken whisper. "I want you to show me."

He kissed her, slow and deep, but she held on after it ended.

"Show me," she repeated, a little more urgently this time. "Now."

"Now?"

"Now."

Mason had planned an afternoon of sightseeing and an early dinner at a five-star French restaurant before heading to the theater to catch *The Lion King*. He'd figured he would work up to seduction with candlelight, soft music, wine and the two-dozen blood-red roses due to be delivered later that evening. He hadn't counted on being seduced.

But he was.

He was seduced by Rose's vulnerability, her straightforwardness, and the undeniable strength that had turned victim into survivor. He'd never realized guts could be sexy. But packaged with Rose's long legs and full lips, they certainly were.

He'd once sworn off rescuing women in distress. But he hadn't rescued Rose. He hadn't needed to. She'd done that all by herself a long time ago. He'd merely had to remind her of that fact, remind her of her worth. In the meantime, she'd returned the favor, showing him that helping people wasn't something to regret. It was who he was, what he was good at. Something he should be proud of.

Mason kissed her with a desperation he'd never felt before.

"You want me to show you right now?" he said, just to be certain he understood her.

"This very minute," she agreed, already reaching for the top button of her blouse. "New York can wait, Mason. This can't."

She had a point, but that didn't mean he'd let her call all of the shots. And he'd had a vivid enough fantasy playing through his head since finding the Victoria's Secret package on his doorstep. He needed to find out if any part of it was possible let alone practical.

"Let me do that," he said, pushing away her hands.

Beneath the blouse, she wore silk. An itty-bitty swatch of pastel blue held up by twin thin strips of lace. One of Victoria's secrets at last revealed. He reached for the waistband of Roz's khaki pants, eager to find out if what she wore beneath them matched the bra and exactly how much of her skin whatever it was managed to cover, but then something occurred to him.

"Wait here," he said, and strode to the door.

"You're leaving? Now?" she asked, incredulous. And well she would be, standing there half-undressed and looking fully aroused.

"Oh, I'm not going anywhere," he assured her and then grinned wickedly. "*Yet.* In the meantime, I don't plan to have any interruptions."

He snatched up the Do Not Disturb sign, opened the door and secured it to the outside knob. Marnie and Bergen might be miles away, but it would be just Mason's luck that housekeeping would pick an inopportune time to turn down the bedding.

"Good thinking," Rose said.

"I was a Boy Scout. We believe in being prepared. Now, where were we?"

"I think right…about…here," Rose said as she unfastened her slacks and did a sexy little shimmy that allowed them to slide down her slender legs to the floor.

*　　*　　*

They spent the better part of the afternoon in bed and that was just fine with Roz. She would have been content to stay tucked under the fluffy comforter and crisp sheets until they had to check out the following day, but Mason was determined to show her some of New York.

"We at least need to eat," he said, pulling the covers away. He waggled his eyebrows at her. "You'll need your strength for later."

Roz laughed but didn't move. Instead she flipped her left arm over her eyes, listening as he moved around the room trying to locate all of his scattered clothing. She needed to regroup. She was exhausted, emotionally and physically. So much was happening to her, inside of her. New feelings and sensations that needed to be sorted, evaluated and understood.

Long ago on the streets, she'd learned that sex could be a weapon. It could be bartered or sold, although Roz had drawn the line against that, even at her most desperate. She'd crossed plenty of lines in her life, redrawn them when necessary, but that one had stayed firm, entrenched and indelible.

Still, she'd had sex before, but what she'd just shared with Mason had been different. Finally she thought she understood why the more poetic referred to it as "making love." She'd always rolled her eyes at that flowery euphemism, but now it seemed the only one to fit. They hadn't spoken of love. For Roz, the words were just too big and scary and new to vocalize at this point. But she'd showed him. She'd poured every bit of her overflowing heart into each kiss and caress, and the look in his eyes as he'd watched her tip over the edge and then shatter like glass told her it was mutual.

It had to be.

"Sweet Mother of God!"

At Mason's exclamation, she bolted upright, holding on for dear life to the covers.

"What! What is it?"

Her gaze darted around the room. She expected to see a video camera or a tarantula or something given the vehemence in his tone. But nothing looked out of place.

Then she realized Mason was staring at her. At her arm.

He rested one knee on the bed and reached for it, turning it over to inspect the small round scars that marched single file from her wrist to just below her elbow.

"Who did this? Who did this to you?"

She pulled back, wishing the room wasn't quite so bright or the old scars quite so white and shiny.

"It's nothing. Just some scars. We both have them," she said, casting a meaningful glance at his shoulder and the remnant of the wound she had gently traced with her tongue half an hour earlier.

"Yes, and you know how I got mine."

She glanced away. "Mason, please. It's the past. It's not important."

"Everything about you is important," he said. Then, he reached out and cupped the side of her face, rubbing the pad of his thumb over her cheek. "Tell me, Rose."

She didn't plan to. What good would it do, exposing every humiliating detail of her childhood? But all that quiet patience in his gaze had the words tumbling from her lips.

"You once asked why I wasn't adopted. And I told you I almost was, by the first family that took me in." And so she told him about the people who had claimed to love her and about their biological son, whose abuse had made it impossible for them to keep her.

Mason didn't offer the usual trite "sorry," and for that she was glad. And it wasn't pity that glazed his expression, but something that seemed oddly akin to admiration. Even so, it made her uncomfortable.

To fill the silence, she told him, "Did you know that when an adoption doesn't work out, they call it a 'disrupted placement.'"

"That's a pretty sanitary term for such an ugly business."

"It wasn't their fault."

"No, and it wasn't yours, either."

He extended her arm so that he could gently kiss each scar and when his lips caressed the final one, Roz accepted at last the truth of those words.

They ate a late lunch at a small bistro not far from the New York Public Library. The place was crowded with boisterous patrons and the scent of freshly baked bread hung thick in the air, making her mouth water long before the harried waitress finally brought their soup and sandwiches.

All through the meal, they talked. Or, rather Mason talked and Roz listened, fascinated by the interesting tidbits he spouted off about New York. Just as the man could identify a bird by its call, he seemed well-versed in the Big Apple's rich history.

"I know you said you'd been to New York before, but how did you know that people once called that skinny building we passed Burnham's Folly? Or that the lion statues at the entrance to the public library are named Patience and Fortitude? I've never met anyone like you." She shook her head in wonder. "You're amazing."

To her surprise, he flushed and then fished a small paperback out of the pocket of his jacket. "Guide book," he muttered.

Roz laughed till her sides ached. "And here I was thinking my boyfriend is a genius."

It was her turn to flush. *Boyfriend.* Was that what he was? The word didn't seem to fit. It didn't seem descriptive enough for his place in her life, for the empty space that he'd filled to nearly bursting in such a short time. But then neither did the more straightforward "guy I'm sleeping with."

"Are you saying I'm not smart?" he

teased. And she was glad he didn't seem as perplexed by her word choice as she was.

"Oh, you're smart. A smart-a—"

"Ah-ah-ah." He shook a finger. "Quit while you're ahead."

On the way back to their hotel, they stopped at the public library. Roz had never seen so many books under one roof. The place was huge and the silence made the atmosphere churchlike. She pulled a book from a shelf, Charlotte Bronte's *Jane Eyre*, and settled at one of the massive oak tables in the library's Main Reading Room where she had agreed to meet Mason. Cracking it open, she read the first line: "There was no possibility of taking a walk that day."

She stumbled over the fourth word because it was so long, but only for a moment. Sounding it out in her head, she smiled with satisfaction.

"What are you doing?" Mason whispered as he settled into the seat opposite her.

"I'm reading," she replied proudly. And his returning smile told her he understood perfectly how much that simple joy meant to her.

The afternoon was winding down, but Roz talked Mason into a visit to the Empire State Building.

"I know that at one point this used to be the world's tallest building," she said.

"For forty years," he nodded. "Did you know it was called the Empty State Building during the Depression because so much of its office space was unrented?"

"Show-off," she muttered as they waited in a queue of tourists for the high-speed elevator.

From the observation deck of the 102nd floor, Roz thought the city looked impersonal and even a bit too tidy. She liked the view from the street better. Not all of the sights or sounds or smells were pleasant, but they were real and, combined, left a definite impression. Kind of like me, she thought.

"Well, I guess we'd better get going if we're going to make *The Lion King*," Roz said as Mason took his turn behind the big viewing scope.

"We'll go tomorrow instead. I don't think I can spend a couple of hours with you in the dark tonight without trying to get you naked. I hear they frown on that at the theater.''

"Tomorrow, but I thought we were going home?''

"Another change of plans, if you don't mind.'' He looked at her over the top of the scope. "I want another day with you here. Another night.''

"I don't mind. Can't say the same about Marnie, though, since she's the one who'll be looking after the tavern.''

Mason shrugged. "We'll bring her back a souvenir.'' His smile was wicked when he added, "I saw a very nice Statue of Liberty hat that would look great on her.''

CHAPTER NINE

IT WAS late Monday afternoon when they returned from their extended weekend. After unpacking, Roz decided to head over to the tavern to return the suitcase Marnie had lent her. And, she knew the other woman would be eager for details from their trip.

Marnie was delivering burgers to Brice Battle and a couple of the other guys from the county road crew when Roz arrived, but that didn't stop Mason's sister from calling out loudly, "Ah, the lovebirds have returned. How was the Big Apple, or should I ask?"

She plucked a French fry from Brice's plate, dipped it into the catsup he'd just squeezed out and told him, "From the way Mason walked in here whistling fifteen minutes ago, they probably never made it outside the hotel room."

Roz rolled her eyes.

"And here we bothered to bring you back a souvenir."

"Did you now? Waldorf-Astoria bath-mat and matching towels?" she teased.

Deciding two could play her game, Roz replied, "Nope. We went all out. And you're going to love it. Come on back to the office when you get a chance and you can try it on."

As Roz had anticipated, Marnie's face lit up like a Christmas tree. "Clothes. You brought me clothes from New York?"

Thinking of the I Love New York T-shirt they'd picked up to go with the Lady Liberty tiara, Roz nodded. "I hope we got the size right."

Marnie grabbed Roz by the arm and all but dragged her back to the storeroom.

"Show me."

"It's nothing much," Roz told her, fishing the gift bag out of the suitcase. Guilt pricked her when she added, "Just something to thank you for tending to the tavern, lending me your luggage and letting me borrow some of your dress clothes."

Marnie dipped her hand eagerly into the bag and, to her credit, even managed to keep the smile pasted on her face when she'd fished out the contents.

"You really didn't have to. *Really,*" she stressed. And then in a martyred tone, she said, "After all, I was happy to help out. And it was really no bother to highlight your hair, manicure your nails and show you how to apply eye shadow and blusher."

"Mason thought you'd get a kick out them," Roz added, laughing.

"I'll get a kick out of something," Marnie replied. "But I have to tell you, Rose, I'm glad this is a joke, otherwise I'd have serious concerns about what you ordered from Victoria's Secret. Not that there's anything in that catalog one can go wrong with."

Roz felt her mouth drop open. "How did you know I ordered something from Victoria's Secret?"

"Small town, sweetheart. My friend Susan is married to the UPS guy."

"So half the town knows where I buy my underwear?" Roz replied, incredulous.

"No. Susan's not terribly discreet and she works at the credit union. Pretty much everyone knows by now and they've all put two and two together, with the lingerie order and the New York trip, and come up with foreplay.''

Roz was mortified, but Marnie was asking, ''So, what did you buy?''

''Bras, panties and this little lacy thing that Mason—'' She broke off, felt her face heat. She couldn't discuss Mason with his sister.

If it bothered Marnie, it didn't show. ''Did you go with the underwire?''

''Um, yeah.''

''What colors?''

''Blue and peach.''

''Which one are you wearing now?''

''Peach.''

''Let me see.''

''Marnie, we hardly know one another,'' Roz teased. She couldn't remember ever having a girlfriend to joke with, share fun secrets with. Show racy underwear to.

With all the authority of a drill sergeant, Marnie ordered, ''Pull up the sweater or drop the pants.''

Roz pulled up the sweater, feeling only marginally foolish when Marnie sighed.

''Cleavage. I knew it. God bless the inventor of the underwire." Marnie's tone was reverent.

And Roz had to agree with her on that score.

Mason walked in just as Roz was smoothing down the hem of her sweater. He didn't know what was going on, but he wasn't sure he liked the gleam in his sister's eye.

"What's up, or should I even ask?"

"Just checking out Rose's new bra," Marnie said baldly. "As I know you have already."

He couldn't think of a thing to say to that, so he stood in the doorway feeling ridiculous. And he knew his sister loved that, too. She patted his flushed face before leaving, and in a voice low enough for only him to hear, said: "She's a keeper, Mason. And it's got nothing to do with the way she fills out a bra."

The weeks passed and the weather turned pleasant and a little more predictable. Sprigs of wintergreen and trailing arbutus dotted the otherwise brown floor of the forest and the big lake was showing signs of thawing, although most of the ice remained.

Roz and Mason traded in skis for walking shoes. He'd tried to talk her into jogging, but to Roz's way of thinking, it just seemed like too much work. So they walked three miles most mornings.

When they reached the halfway point of their trek on this day, Mason again tried to coax her into a trot. He ran a few steps ahead, then turned and jogged in place while she walked to where he was.

"Come on, Rose. This will help strengthen your muscles, give them nice definition."

She took a moment to admire his legs through the nylon jogging pants he wore. Of course, she also knew what they looked like without any covering. Very defined. Very fine.

"You're smiling. Is that a yes?"

"I'm smiling because…never mind. And no, I haven't changed my mind. Have you ever seen anyone who looks happy while they're running? They all look like they're in pain."

"It's good for you," he countered again.

"So's liver and even when I was half-starved, I wouldn't touch the stuff."

He fell into step beside her. "It's hard to think of you as going hungry."

A smile bloomed on her face, and he wondered if she realized how often she did that lately, or the effect it always had on his pulse rate.

"Is that your subtle way of letting me know you noticed the ten pounds I've gained since I've been here?"

Oh, he'd noticed the added weight all right. And he had no complaints. Rose was still too thin to his way of thinking, but her lean figure now had delicate curves in places that drew Mason's attention as well as his hands. That wasn't what he meant, though.

He frowned. "This is America. People aren't supposed to go hungry here."

"Because it's the land of plenty?"

"Yes."

"But people do go hungry here. And sometimes they're homeless, too. I'm proof of that," she said quietly. "Living, breathing proof."

"Well, there should be a safety net."

"There is, Mason, but it doesn't catch

everyone. Just as a free public education doesn't guarantee that every child in this country will learn how to read. The poor, the homeless, the semiliterate, we don't have a lot of clout with the people who make the laws and divvy up the money because, generally, we don't vote. You need to be able to read a ballot to vote. You need an address to register. I haven't had one of those—a permanent one—since I've been old enough to cast a ballot and have my say.''

''Are you trying to tell me something, Rose?''

''No. I'm not like Marnie, even though I know her heart's in the right place. I won't push and bully you into doing something you don't want to do. You have your reasons for not wanting to enter politics. I respect them.''

''But?''

''But I think you have incredible passion.'' When he smiled lasciviously, she narrowed her eyes. ''I'm talking about outside of the bedroom in this case.''

''Well, passion's not enough. You need endorsements, connections and money. *Lots* of money. Representatives run every two years, meaning you're literally running for reelection all of the time.''

''Except during the third term in office.''

She saw the surprise in his expression and didn't know whether to be pleased by it or put out.

''Term limits.'' She shrugged. ''I've been picking up the newspaper now and then, trying to read it. And, of course, the television in the tavern is on all the time.''

''Well, you might be able to put conviction and principle ahead of politics as a lame duck, but even most term-limited lawmakers have their eye on another office. They're already running for the state Senate at that point or national office. Or maybe they've decided to switch sides and lobby for the special interests. There's a lot of money to be made there.''

''Is that what you would do?''

''Of course not. I'm just saying the system is far from perfect.'' He sighed wearily. ''Not quite broken, but sometimes I think damn close.''

''So, the system's not perfect.'' She shrugged. ''But your sister is right. *You* would be a perfect lawmaker because your heart would be in the right place. You'd have to bend now and then. After all, little gets done without compromising. But you'd never sell out. I think that's one of the things I love most about you.''

She colored after she said that. And he felt his heart beat in triple time. Since returning from New York, they hadn't spent a night apart. They slept together in his bed, cuddled beneath his down comforter, making love and then often talking into the wee hours of the morning. But neither one of them had used the actual word for what was happening between them.

Now she had.

He stopped walking, grabbing her hand to make her stop as well. And because he wasn't quite sure how to respond, he decided to ask, ''What else do you love about me, Rose?''

He expected some sop to his ego, maybe a clever switch in topics or even a skewing barb, but when she replied, her quietly spoken words staggered him.

''You look at me. You have, right from the first day when you picked me up on the side of the highway. You look me right in the eye when you speak to me, when I speak to you. And you *see* me.''

"You're pretty hard to miss," he said, tipping his head down to kiss her cheek.

"No, I'm not. I've often felt like the guy in that book we read last week. The one by Ralph Ellison."

"The Invisible Man," Mason supplied.

"Yes. I know people can see me, but they often chose not to. Oh, sure, they saw me just fine when I walked into a store. Raggedy jacket, torn jeans. 'Keep an eye on that one. She might try to swipe something.' But to the state I was a number and to some of my foster families, I was a paycheck. To the schools, I was a nuisance who helped drag down the standardized test scores. They never saw Roz Bennett, let alone Rose."

"Don't cry."

"I'm not," she said. But then realized her cheeks were wet, her throat clogged with the emotions she finally felt safe enough to voice.

"I love you, Mason. I think I started falling in love with you the first time you called me Rose. You *see* me," she repeated.

He wiped away her tears, blinked his own moist eyes. "I love you, too."

*   *   *

Rose had never been happier. That's how she'd come to think of herself now as well.

Rose. Rose Bennett.

No more Roz. Roz was the tough-talking itinerant with the boy-short hair and the aimless, restless feet.

Rose could read, her hair was still short but styled and highlighted blond now, and she was no longer restless, aimless or itinerant. She had direction in life and, for the first time, roots. Shallow, but there. Sinking down into the fertile ground of Chance Harbor. She'd even registered to vote. Mason had taken her to the Secretary of State office, where the process was accomplished quickly and easily now that she had a permanent address.

Last Chance Harbor, Mason had once told her some people called the small town. And now she thought that apropos even if he'd been referring to the sailors on Superior at the time.

All around her, nature was renewing itself. The trees' tight buds were beginning to loosen. The robins had returned, strutting across Mason's yard in their quest for worms. She'd spotted wildflowers in the woods behind the tavern. Trillium, Mason told her. And trout lily, violets, yellow lady slippers and bloodroot.

She felt renewed as well, and beautiful. In a book about wildflowers that she'd checked out of the public library, she found a picture of a wild iris called a blue flag. Its blossom was gorgeous, the thin curving petals downright delicate. And yet it grew in swamps.

Rose liked the idea that something that looked that lovely could grow in such an unlikely place. It gave her hope.

And just as she had changed, so had Mason. On the very day Rose's voter registration card arrived in the mail, he surprised her and Marnie by announcing he planned to run for the state House of Representatives.

He said the gaps in the child welfare system had to be filled, and he'd decided to make it his business to see that they were. He could do that best, he said, as a member of the Legislature.

Representative Mason Striker. Rose thought it had a nice ring.

She was whistling when she walked into the tavern just before her shift. And she was smiling when she spotted Mason behind the vast sweep of mahogany.

"I've got good news," he called out when he saw her.

She took a fistful of beer nuts and before dropping them into her mouth, asked, "What might that be?"

"I think I've found your mother."

She choked on the nuts. Coughing in dramatic fashion before she could muster up, "What?"

"Let's go back to the office," Mason said. Then he called to his sister, "Marnie, mind the tap for a bit."

She collapsed into the chair behind his desk when the door closed behind them. Good news, he'd said. But was it?

"You think you found her?"

"I've been following a lead for a few weeks now. I didn't want to tell you in case it didn't pan out. But it looks like it has. Her name is Delores. Delores Kingsley Treller. She's only forty-two, which places her at about sixteen when you were born."

Rose absorbed the information, or rather tried to, but she heard only the numbers sixteen and forty-two, and thought about the wide gap between them.

"She was probably scared out of her wits. Raising a child is a lot of responsibility, especially when you're just a kid yourself."

He was trying to make her feel better, trying to make excuses for the woman who had brought Rose into the world and then abandoned her to it. And she loved him all the more because of it.

"Where is she now?"

"California."

"And I was heading west," Rose mused. "What happens now?"

"I've got a flight out to San Diego in the morning."

"Alone?"

He took her hand, gave it a squeeze. "I think it's for the best, Rose. If this turns out to be a dead end, I'd rather not have dragged you across the country on a wild-goose chase."

"And if she's really the one?"

"She'll still be the one when I get back, then you both can decide how you want to meet."

"Or if," Rose added. "She may not want to see me. She could have looked,

Mason. I was in the system for nearly fifteen years.''

"Well, you'll have some of your answers regardless. You'll know what she named you."

"That doesn't matter to me now," she said slowly. "I used to wonder, but now I don't really care. I'm Rosalind Bennett. I'm Rose."

"Yes," Mason said. "That's exactly who you are."

It was foggy when Mason's plane took off from the airport in Houghton. Foggy and spitting rain. Rose tried not to think of that as a bad omen, but it was hard not to.

She'd stood in the airport hugging Mason close before he boarded the commuter jet that would take him to Chicago's O'Hare Airport. From there he would fly to California. Part of her didn't want to let him go.

Even now, as she drove Mason's Jeep back to Chance Harbor, she couldn't help but wonder if she wouldn't be better off leaving the past alone. She didn't need the answers as desperately as she once had. She knew who she was now. And even if

she didn't quite have family, she had people who cared about her, loved her. People
who counted regardless of any blood tie.
People who thought she mattered.

Couldn't that be enough?

As the Jeep's speedometer nudged past
sixty miles per hour on the lonely stretch
of highway, Rose pushed one of Mason's
hard-edged rock CDs into the vehicle's
player and cranked up the volume.

Stephen Tyler's voice hissed out of the
speakers as he belted out one of
Aerosmith's vintage tunes. And Rose
hoped the music would bludgeon away her
concerns.

CHAPTER TEN

ON THE long flight from San Diego to Chicago, Mason agonized over what he should do. Should he tell Rose what he'd discovered about her mother?

All of it?

Any of it?

It wasn't that he didn't think she couldn't handle hearing the unvarnished truth. As far as he could tell, she was a pro at handling heartbreak. But in this case, what purpose would it serve?

As he boarded the aircraft that would take him from Chicago to Houghton, he was no closer to figuring out what he would do when his plane touched down and he once again stood face-to-face with the woman he loved.

Oh, he'd found Delores Kingsley, now Delores Treller, all right. She was married to an investment banker and living quite

nicely in a swank suburban San Diego
neighborhood.

When he'd arrived at her home the day
before, she'd been in the front yard, tending to a flower bed. He'd sat in his rental
car across the street, and, since his visit was
unexpected, snapped a few pictures.

At forty-two, she was still a knockout,
the wildness of her youth tamed by weekly
gym workouts, expensive spa treatments
and a little BOTOX, as he'd discovered
with a few discreet inquiries around town.
A tumble of blond hair spilled from beneath the straw hat that shaded her fair
complexion and she clutched a pair of
pruning shears in one gloved hand. She was
snipping back the branches of a bush. A
rosebush, Mason realized, with sudden un-
ease.

He got out of the car and walked toward
her, noting other similarities to Rose as he
approached: Same long legs and slender
build. Same high cheekbones and full
mouth.

She'd smiled at him at first, politely and
with mild curiosity. And he'd glimpsed his
Rose in another decade and a half in those
full, upturned lips. But the smile evapo-

rated as soon as he explained who he was and the purpose of his visit.

Very quickly, Mason realized the vast differences between the woman he loved and the woman who shared her DNA.

Delores Kingsley Treller looked him right in the eye and, without so much as blinking, informed him, ''That business is the past.''

She kept her voice lowered, presumably concerned about being overheard by gossipy neighbors and the two teenage girls who were in the driveway of her hacienda-style home washing a convertible. Like Rose and their mother, the girls were blond and slender. He gauged them to be about thirteen and fifteen. Neither looked old enough to drive the pricey late-model Mercedes they were busily scrubbing with soapy sponges.

Rose had half sisters, two of them. And yet, even now, it was clear that her mother wanted nothing to do with her.

Mason wasn't letting Delores Kingsley Treller off the hook so easily. She'd walked away once before. He wasn't going to let her do it this time. Not before he had the answers Rose wanted. The answers she needed and deserved.

"Look at your daughter."

He held up one of the snapshots he'd taken of Rose in New York City. She was smiling—beaming actually—as she stood atop the Empire State Building. The wind had turned her cheeks pink and left her hair an adorable mess. She looked beautiful, happy and, to Mason, a whole different person from the bedraggled, half-starved waif he'd picked up on the side of the highway back in February.

But the woman in front of him only scowled at the photograph and then pushed it away with one of her gloved hands, as if the sight of the smiling young woman was simply too much to tolerate.

"I made a mistake, Mr. Striker."

"It's Mason. And I'd say it was more than a mistake."

She glanced nervously over her shoulder and lowered her voice to just above a whisper.

"I was sixteen at the time and not living in the best situation. When Crystal came along—"

"Crystal?" He groaned and closed his

eyes briefly. Mason had been a cop in Detroit long enough to know a lot of junkies named their kids after their drug of choice. He wanted to be wrong about this, prayed he was when he asked, "Let me guess: cocaine?"

She gave a jerky nod and his stomach lurched.

"And later crack. I had a serious drug problem. And I was already in deep to a dealer. I owed him a bundle and I...I needed a fix."

She licked her lips, as if remembering the desperate need she'd experienced. And Mason felt sorry for her, or rather for the lost teenager she'd been at the time.

"We came to an understanding." Her gaze darted away. "We, um, settled on an exchange of sorts."

"You sold yourself for drugs," Mason stated bluntly as bitterness filled his mouth. He hadn't thought what he discovered about Rose's past could get worse, but it did. "You traded sex for, what, a five-dollar rock of crack and then you wound up pregnant?"

Part of him hoped the woman would dispute his ugly assertion, but she didn't.

Standing in front of him wearing her crisp cotton walking shorts, sleeveless blouse and a pair of impossibly white Keds, she looked poised and polished and far removed from the gritty streets of Detroit.

During his preliminary investigation, Mason had discovered that Delores Kingsley had grown up in privilege—so close and yet a world away from the intersection where she'd ultimately abandoned Rose. Take Jefferson Avenue far enough east, he recalled from his days on the Detroit police force, from his days of watching over Amelia, and the graffiti-decorated buildings of the city gave way to the well-appointed estates of Lake Shore Drive in nearby Grosse Pointe.

Delores's parents lived in one of those mansions with its view of Lake St. Clair. But she'd been more of a guest. They paid handsomely to have their only daughter educated at an exclusive all-girl academy on the East Coast, where she boarded for nine months of the year. Delores Kingsley was the stereotypical poor little rich girl. She'd craved excitement and begged for attention from her family. Now, as the last pieces of the puzzle fell into place, Mason realized that she'd found both when she'd gotten hooked on drugs.

It reminded him a little too much of the situation with Amelia, and it struck him as tragically bizarre that both he and Rose had wound up casualties of other people's drug addictions.

And some people still thought that using was harmless or only harmful to the person getting high, he thought bitterly.

"My parents disowned me. They said as long as I was taking drugs, I wasn't welcome in their home and they wouldn't pay the tuition at the school I attended in Connecticut."

"So you ran away."

"Yes. I was living in a drug house when Crystal came along. I didn't even realize I was pregnant until…"

"Until it was too late to do anything about it?"

She lifted her chin, but didn't quite look him in the eye, and he had his answer. She would have had an abortion if time had been on her side. Thank God it hadn't been.

Faint color splotched her cheeks, but she was a cool one as she tucked the shears into one of her pockets and then slowly peeled off her pristine gardening gloves.

"I tried to make a life for us at first, but it was hard and my parents remained... estranged. I had to make some choices. I'll admit that some of them were poor ones."

"Poor choices!" Mason thundered, unable to let her sanitize the past—Rose's past, which had been littered with so much refuse and debris.

"Lower your voice!" she pleaded. Then waved and smiled brightly at her daughters, who'd stopped scrubbing the car and were now eyeing Mason suspiciously.

"Everything okay, Mom?" the older one called.

"Yes, honey, fine." To Mason she said, "I think you should leave."

"Not yet," he said, but he did lower his voice. "I've got something to say to you and you'll damn well listen. You abandoned your daughter on a street corner in Detroit. You left a toddler wandering around near traffic wearing little more than a diaper in the dead of winter. You could have gone through legal—not to mention safe—channels to terminate your parental rights. Your child deserved that much at least. And even though you were young, it was within your power to do it for her. You took the easy way out, and she suffered because of it.''

''I don't know how much you and the girl want, Mr. Striker, but I'll pay it.''

''Your *daughter* doesn't want money,'' he snapped, outraged on Rose's behalf that the woman could think this was all about a check. ''She wants answers, maybe even a chance to meet with you.''

She wants love.

''Oh, no.'' She backed up a step. ''Absolutely not. I have a new life now. I'm clean. I have been since—''

''Let me guess. Since you dumped your daughter and went home to Mommy and Daddy.''

''They agreed to pay for my rehabilitation,'' she said stiffly. ''I was nineteen and my life wasn't going anywhere. My parents gave me a second chance and I took it. You'll not make me feel guilty for that.''

''But they didn't want your daughter. That would be too hard to explain to their pals at the yacht club, eh?''

''Go ahead and act self-righteous, Mr. Striker. I did what I had to do then and I'll do what I have to do now. If you or the girl tries to contact me again, I'll file a stalking complaint with the police. They take that offense very seriously in California.''

He huffed out a breath. "So, that's it?"

"I'm sorry, but yes. My mind is made up. It has been for twenty-three years.''

Mason started to turn away, then stopped. "Was it really that easy to cut her loose?"

She swallowed and he glimpsed what he hoped was regret. But her gaze glittered hard and resolute when she replied, "It was for the best.''

"For the best? You might want to ask your daughter about that. She bounced around in Michigan's foster care system for nearly fifteen years. And since then she's lived hand-to-mouth to survive. And she has survived.''

"You might not believe this, but I'm glad.''

"Not glad enough to meet with her, though. Or to introduce her to her half sisters.'' He motioned toward the girls in the driveway.

Panic widened her eyes. "They have nothing to do with Crystal.''

"Rose, her name is Rose now. And she might disagree." He shook his head, saddened, sickened. Parents weren't supposed to be like this.

"I love your daughter, Mrs. Treller. She's beautiful, smart, funny. Doesn't any of that matter to you?"

"I…I'm glad she's okay," Delores said briskly as she pulled back on her gardening gloves. And the symbolism was hard to miss. She didn't want to soil her hands.

"But?"

"But that doesn't change the facts. My husband doesn't know about my past, Mr. Striker. Neither do my two daughters. And I plan to keep it that way."

"Fine." Mason shook his head in disgust. "I've got the answers I came for anyway. But just for the record, ma'am. You have *three* daughters."

Now, as the small airplane taxied to a stop in Houghton, Mason wasn't so sure he did have all of the answers he'd sought. And, he knew for certain that he didn't have any answers Rose would appreciate hearing.

* * *

She was waiting when he emerged from the gate. Marnie stood with her, but his gaze went to Rose and stayed there. She wore a red blouse with lipstick to match. Her jeans were new and a little on the tight side, accenting the subtle flair of her hips and the long line of her legs. A pair of simple gold earrings winked at him when she tilted her head to one side and smiled slowly. Marnie's doing, all of it. But then he had no doubt Rose would have bloomed without any fussing from his sister.

She was happy now, settled. Perfect. And Mason wanted her to stay that way. Mind made up, he walked faster, nearly running, and when he reached her, he pulled her hard into his arms. Without a care for who might be watching, Mason kissed her thoroughly until he heard his sister's discreet cough.

He ended the kiss, but he didn't let Rose go. He never would, he realized.

"I missed you," he whispered.

"So the whole world gathers," Marnie said dryly before Rose had a chance to catch her breath.

Something seemed wrong to Rose. Something about the way Mason still held her so tightly, as if to protect her or absorb some sort of blow on her behalf. And she had to know, right then, what he'd discovered on his trip. It couldn't wait until they reached the Jeep and began the trip back to Chance Harbor.

"What is it, Mason? What did you find out?"

"Let's get out of here first."

"No, I need to know now, please. Before we take another step."

He glanced at Marnie, then back at Rose, looking torn.

"It's not the best news," he said slowly.

She gave a jerky nod. "I gathered that, which means it won't get any better during the ride home."

He led her to a bank of chairs and gently pushed her into one before he squatted down in front of her. Marnie sat next to her, twining her fingers through the ones on Rose's left hand in a gesture of support that was more than appreciated.

"She doesn't want anything to do with me, is that it?"

Mason appeared to search for the right words. She'd never seen him like this, so cautious, so nervous.

"It's not that. She's...she's...your mother is dead, Rose," he blurted out at last. "I'm sorry."

"Dead?" It came as a blow, a surprisingly painful one. "When? How?"

"A car accident, just a week ago, which is why I didn't know about it before I went to California. But I got a chance to talk to a neighbor. I got some of the answers for you. And I got this."

He pulled a Polaroid from his pocket and handed it to her.

It was a candid shot of a woman standing in a lush front yard tending to flowers. She looked happy, pretty. And even though Rose still had a million questions, she at last had a face to put with the title of mother.

"She's beautiful, Rose," Marnie said, giving her hand a squeeze. "And you look just like her."

Emotion clogged her throat for a moment. She wasn't sure what she should feel. How could she grieve for someone she didn't know? For someone she had long ago told herself she hated? And was it wrong to feel let down that she wouldn't be able to confront her mother now? Was it wrong to be sad that she wouldn't have all of the answers she'd so recently begun to seek in earnest?

"What else did you find out?"

"Um...she and her husband lived quietly, but the neighbors liked them."

Rose glanced up. "She was married. Did, does she have other children?"

"Um, no." He shook his head, looked away. "No other children."

"Any idea why she left me?" she asked.

"Well, she was quite chummy with one of the neighbors. I spoke to the woman at length, explained the reason for my visit. She said your mother had spoken about you in confidence a couple of times. She—that is, the neighbor, said that your mother really regretted what had happened, but she'd been young and scared at the time. She said your mother hoped that you were okay and that, wherever you were, you were happy and had forgiven her for abandoning you."

"Really?"

"Yes, really. That's *exactly* what she said."

He gripped her hands as if to give his words more importance than they already had. "She loved you, Rose. In her own way, I'm sure that your mother loved you. How could she not?"

She nodded once. Then again. "Well, now I know, right?"

"Right," Marnie said.

"Now you know," Mason repeated. But something about his expression looked haunted, guilty even.

She shook off the thought. What would Mason have to feel guilty about? It wasn't his fault her mother was dead.

"Let's go home," Marnie said.

Home. With Mason's arm wrapped around her shoulders and Marnie still holding her hand, Rose could think of no sweeter destination.

CHAPTER ELEVEN

SUMMER arrived, and with it carloads of tourists, mostly from downstate. The locals called the folks from Michigan's Lower Peninsula trolls, since they came from "under the bridge." The nickname was generally affectionate and a payback of sorts for being tapped as yoopers, as in U.P., the abbreviation for Upper Peninsula.

Rose proudly considered herself a full-fledged yooper now. She hardly noticed anymore when she, too, sprinkled her sentences with the characteristic "eh?"

She also considered herself a full-fledged member of the Chance Harbor community. She had her own library card, mailing address and, at Marnie's urging, she had even joined the town's Beautification Committee, which really just meant she helped plant pansies in the flower boxes outside the shops near the main section of town. Still, it made her feel part of something. Just as Mason and Marnie made her feel part of something.

A family.

Her status as a Striker was hardly official, but Marnie referred to her as "Aunt Rose" when she spoke lovingly to the baby growing in her slightly rounded tummy, and she often poked at Mason about trading in his bachelorhood for married life so he and Rose could give her baby a cousin to play with.

For now, Rose told herself that was enough. She didn't need a ring or a white dress or bouquet of orange blossoms. She didn't need to stand at the front of the little white church she and Mason attended on Sundays and make promises before God and their guests. Mason loved her, wanted her. That alone was a miracle to savor.

Even as she thought this, though, she knew something between them had changed. She'd noticed it right after his return from California. She couldn't quite put a finger on what it was. He hadn't pulled back exactly. They still made love every night, sometimes almost desperately it seemed to her. And at times she would catch him watching her, a considering look

in his eye. Or he'd start to say something—
something she would swear was important—only to change his mind or the subject.

"It's nothing," he would say.

Nothing was starting to make her worry.

But she didn't have a lot of time to fret,
because the pace of life picked up along
with the temperature. Tourists filled the
state campground on the outer edge of
Chance Harbor and kept the motel's neon
No Vacancy sign blinking proudly each
weekend and, with the Fourth of July ap-
proaching, even most weekdays. Blankets
and shade umbrellas dotted the public
beaches, even though Superior was hardly
a gracious host and never warmed up
enough for its guests to enjoy more than a
quick dip in its icy waters.

The rocky beach not far from the lighthouse was inhospitable and largely private,
so Rose preferred to spend the early afternoon there when she could, soaking up a
little sunshine and listening to the peaceful
music of the waves.

She could read now, well enough to pick
up a paperback on her own and actually
enjoy the story. And she loved watching

the big freighters press through the open water farther out, carrying their heavy loads of taconite and iron ore from Wisconsin.

She was watching a freighter pass on this sunny afternoon when a shadow fell across her. She glanced up into Bergen's creased, scowling face.

"Boss wants to know if you can get your bony butt to work a couple hours early today. Marnie's not feeling well."

She ignored his comment about her posterior and asked, "She okay?"

"Just baby tired is all," he offered grudgingly. "Been doing too much lately, if you ask me."

"We ought to tie her into a chair next time she shows up at the tavern," Rose muttered. "That's about the only way to keep her off her feet."

Bergen surprised her by grunting out what sounded like a laugh, and for the first time in memory he actually agreed with her. "Ain't that the truth?"

"Tell Mason I just need to change my clothes and I'll be right over."

She stood and collected her blanket and book, dumping out the warm remnants of her cola as she started up the rocky path that led to the lighthouse.

She nearly tripped and tumbled backward when she heard the surly cook reply, "Okay, *Rose*."

Rose was humming when she entered the tavern. And when she walked into the kitchen to grab a clean apron off one of the pegs, she felt giddy enough to grin at Bergen.

"That smile's not going to get you a French fry before break, girlie," he snarled.

"Oh, you like me, Bergen. Come on, admit it."

"Too much sun," he muttered sourly. "You've become delusional."

"I heard you call me Rose."

"So? It's your name, ain't it?"

"Don't worry," she said and felt confident enough to pat his weathered cheek. "I won't tell anyone."

"Get out of my kitchen," he snapped, but there was no real bite to his words. And he didn't even try to swat her hand away when she sneaked it into the warming tray and stole a fry.

Out in the hallway, she caught a glimpse

of Mason sitting at his desk when she passed the open door to his office. He had the phone pressed to one ear and a harassed look on his handsome face.

"Good, you came early," he said, holding the receiver away from his mouth. "I'm on hold with one of our beer distributors. They screwed up our order." He rolled his eyes. "Last thing I need today."

"I saw the woman from the state Democratic Party out front. Anything I can do before I start waiting tables?"

He swore under his breath. "Diane's already here?"

Rose nodded. "Walked in just ahead of me. I set her up with a glass of iced tea. She's fine for the moment."

"Yeah, but I don't want to keep her waiting and these guys have me on permahold." He motioned to the phone with his free hand.

"I can handle the call for you," Rose offered. "Just tell me what I need to do."

He grinned his relief and kissed her cheek after he handed her the receiver.

"You're an angel. Just go over the order with them again. It's pretty much the same as it's been for the past couple of months.

File's in the top drawer if you need to look at it. Quincy Brothers Distributing.

At the door, he stopped, turned and, running a hand through his hair, asked, "Do I look okay?"

"Okay?"

She ran her tongue over her teeth. Oh, nothing quite so bland as that adjective, she decided, noting the sexy ruffled hair, the chiseled lines of his cheeks, the incisive gaze that, when it landed on her, always left her feeling stripped bare. And she felt it again, that fierce kick of physical attraction that had heat seeping through her system.

"I could get arrested for what I'm thinking," she said, only half teasing. And still amazed that even when the desire cooled a bit, the warmth stayed.

Raising one eyebrow in speculation, he replied, "Oh? Well, hold that thought till I can do something about it." Then asked again, "So, how do I look?"

"Like a man of the people."

And she blew him a kiss for luck.

When he was gone, Rose pulled open the drawer and thumbed through the hanging files. She was still on hold, listening to an instrumental version of Barry Manilow's "Mandy" and so she thought she understood perfectly why Mason had looked so pained when she'd first stepped into his office.

If she recalled right, it was Z-17 on the jukebox. She'd have to play it later, just to really cap his day. Smiling, she pulled out the file she sought, inadvertently grabbing two at the same time. When she went to replace the other one, the name on the tab stopped her.

Delores Kingsley Treller.

Mason had made up a file on her mother. Rose grinned. How like him. The man was too organized for his own good. She opened it expecting to read the same limited information Mason had passed on to her. But there was more here.

Much, much more, including her legal name: Crystal Marie Kingsley, and several paragraphs of notes penned in Mason's slashing script that detailed the circumstances surrounding her birth and what her mother's lifestyle had been at the time.

As she read the words a moan escaped her lips and her stomach grew queasy. She'd been born to a drug addict. Her father had been her mother's dealer. Sex for drugs, with a little unexpected bonus nine months later, she thought, swallowing back the bile that crept up her throat.

She hadn't expected her biological parents to be Ozzie and Harriet Nelson. She hadn't even expected them to be married or perfectly upstanding citizens.

But this?

Born as the result of a drug transaction? It was almost too much to bear. Almost too much for her new sense of self-esteem to withstand.

Even before she could begin to absorb the pain of that, she spied the photographs. They were not just of her mother, but of two girls. Two teenage girls who bore a striking resemblance to Rose.

And it hit her, quite literally staggered her so that she had to grip the edge of the desk to keep from tipping forward out of her seat: Mason had lied to her.

Rose had sisters. Two of them. Younger sisters whom he'd seen during his trip to California. She scanned the rest of the information, looking for a death notice or some notation of her mother's fatal car wreck. But she found nothing, nothing at all until she looked into the margin and spied "refuses to meet" tucked sideways and underscored twice.

"Can I help you?"

The voice came from the telephone, which she realized she still held to one ear.

"No." No one can, she thought, as she hung up and then plunged both hands into her hair.

Her mother was alive and perfectly healthy, living a clean and comfortable life in suburban San Diego. In the photos, she looked like the stereotypical soccer mom, wearing white canvas shoes, a Mercedes in the driveway along with those two perfect daughters.

And all the while her third daughter was tucked safely away in the closet.

Forgotten.

Forgettable.

And Mason. Mason had lied to her. He had lied to her about *everything*. Even her mother's rejection didn't cut Rose as deeply as that fact. After all, Delores Kingsley had never claimed to love Rose.

She shook her head, tried to clear it and think. There had to be reasons, very good reasons, why Mason had kept all of this

vital, life-altering information to himself.
Rose stood and, though her legs still felt
shaky, she walked to the door. She would
ask him. She would simply ask him.

When she rounded the corner of the bar,
she spied him sitting with Diane Sutherland
at a table in the corner. Their heads were
bent toward one another and they were
deep in conversation, no doubt plotting
campaign strategy since both political par-
ties considered this legislative district key
to gaining control of the closely divided
House in the upcoming election. It promised to be one hell of a race since the district's voters leaned Democratic by only a
couple of percentage points.

Rose stumbled to a halt, understanding
plunking into place even as the bottom
dropped out of her happy new world.

Oh, Mason had a good reason to keep
her past buried, all right. And she thought
she knew exactly what it was. She recalled
what he'd told her about Senator Bertrand,
the distinguished federal legislator from
Michigan who had hired Mason to watch
over his wayward daughter. The man was
a political legend, a campaign strategist's
dream come true. He knew which sound

bites to utter, which talking points to punch. And he knew that ugly personal revelations could sabotage one's political ambitions.

What could be uglier than dallying with the illegitimate daughter of a crack addict and a drug dealer? Even Rose's being homeless and semiliterate were attractive qualities by comparison.

And then another blow landed. Could Mason be ashamed of her? Or maybe just ashamed to be attracted to someone whose origins were so squalid, sordid?

She retraced her steps to his office, sank down in the chair behind the desk. She glanced again at the photographs and Mason's notes, but soon couldn't see them through the haze of her tears.

The roots she'd put down in Chance Harbor over the past several months weren't so deep that they couldn't be torn out, but they were plenty deep enough that doing so would be painful. Yet, if there was one thing Rose knew it was that she couldn't stay. And because she knew this, she mourned.

"Hey, it's getting busy out there,"

Mason said as he opened the door. "Are you...Rose? What is it?"

Brows tugging together in concern, he quickly closed the door and crossed to where she sat.

"What's wrong, sweetheart?"

She knuckled away her tears, hating the weakness they represented and yet unable to stop them.

"I found the file." Holding it up, she added, "My sisters look a lot like me, don't you think?"

His face bleached of color and he had the grace to look both guilty and contrite.

"Let me explain."

"Explain why you told me my mother was dead? Or why you told me I didn't have any other family when it turns out I have sisters. Two of them? Damn you!"

But the oath came out more as a sob.

"You of all people knew what finding her, finding a family, meant to me. I trusted you. I *loved* you."

"Don't say it like that. Like it's in the past tense."

"What kind of future can we have when you're ashamed of me?"

"Ashamed of you?"

"I'm a drug addict's daughter, Mason." She snorted out a laugh. "Named Crystal, for crying out loud. You were a cop. You must have thought, how cliché. Maybe you're ashamed to be attracted to someone like me."

"I'm not ashamed of you. Think whatever else you want about my motives, Rose, but not that."

"Okay, so you're not ashamed of me, just acting in your own best interests. I saw you out there with Diane, making your plans for election. Maybe she even knows about my past and has suggested that you can champion people like me, but the public doesn't need to know you actually *sleep* with people like me. That won't grab votes, especially among conservative swing voters. And that's who you'll need to ensure your election."

He reached for her, but she backed away so that his fingers merely grazed her elbow.

"You can't think that."

"What am I supposed to think? You didn't want me to go with you to California. Were you worried about what you would find?"

"Yes, but not for the reasons you're accusing me of. And if you love me—if you love me half as much as I love you—you *know* that.''

His words tugged at her. She wanted to believe them, but a lifetime of experience had her stepping back, stepping away.

''I have to go.''

''Go where?''

''Out. Away. I need to think.''

''Don't do this, Rose. Don't give in to the past now when we have a future.''

His voice was loud as thunder, and it followed her as she raced out the door.

It was half past eleven when she walked into the tavern the following morning just as Mason was preparing to call the state police and report her missing. He'd spent a sleepless night pacing the floors of the lighthouse, worry and anger warring with one another as he wondered where in the hell she could be.

Now she stood in front of him, looking cool and remote. And he knew that more than aged mahogany separated the two of them.

''Rose, thank God!'' Marnie cried, coming over to give her a quick hug. In uncharacteristic fashion, however, his meddling sister retreated right afterward.

When she was gone, Mason said, ''I've been worried about you.''

''Sorry about that, but I needed time to think.''

''Couldn't do that and make a phone call, eh?''

''Sorry,'' she said again.

She'd come to a decision, he could see that in the way she held herself: chin up, shoulders squared, feet firmly planted. And the likelihood was good he wasn't going to agree with what she had to say.

''Want to go in back so we can talk?'' she asked.

He glanced around at the sparse crowd of regulars. The Battle brothers were already chalking up their cues, preparing for their first pool game of the day. A few other guys from the county road crew were sipping colas and talking trash. Big Bob Bailey was at the other end of the bar, his usual whiskey neat in his hand. And Marnie was sitting with her feet up for a change, but he didn't doubt for a moment that her ears were attuned to every word being spoken.

"We can talk out here. It's all *family.*" He used the word intentionally and was rewarded with her wince.

"I'd rather talk in private."

"Why? I know what you're going to say. You're leaving." It came out as an accusation, because it was. "You're pulling up stakes and cutting out because that's what you do best when the going gets tough. But I resent like hell that you're doing it without giving me an opportunity to explain."

"Fine." She crossed her arms. "Explain now. Explain why you didn't tell me the truth."

"You read the file, Rose. That should be obvious. I wanted to protect you. I didn't want you to be hurt." He lowered his voice. "She...she doesn't want to meet you. She threatened to go to the police, file a stalking complaint if we so much as tried to contact her or her new family again. How could I tell you that? How could I look the woman I love square in the eye and tell her..."

"That my own mother doesn't want me," she finished for him, her tone flat and loud enough to carry to every occupant of the room. "But I already knew that,

Mason. I've known that for twenty-three years.''

"It still has to hurt. I thought I could spare you that.''

"And I thought you were different. But you're just like all of the caseworkers and foster parents and school counselors who popped in and out of my life over the years. They all *knew* what was best for me although none of them ever bothered to ask me what I thought, what I wanted.''

"I'm asking now. What do you want, Rose?''

"Maybe you should call me Roz,'' she said wearily. "You can't change my life story, you can't change my name and you can't change me.''

"I didn't change you. You changed yourself. Just as I've changed since I've known you. And you are Rose,'' he insisted. "I know who you are.''

"I'm the illegitimate daughter of—''

"No!'' he shouted. "And you're really starting to tick me off. That's not who you are. I know it and you know it. Whatever name you choose to go by, I'll love you, because I fell in love with the person, not with your name or with your past. I fell in love with you and I want you. I want the whole package, baggage and all. And I want it for keeps.''

She'd never seen Mason like this. Irritated, impatient. And his vehemence convinced Rose that he had acted out of love in keeping his findings from her. He might have chosen a foolish way of showing it, but his intentions had been honorable.

And old-fashioned, she realized when he flipped up the hinged section of the bar and got down on one knee in front of her.

''Oh, my God!'' she heard Marnie cry. And Brice Battle moaned something that sounded like ''Poor S.O.B.''

But Mason wasn't put off. Not by Rose's stunned silence, not by their gaping audience.

''This isn't exactly the way I planned to do this. I planned a romantic evening, candlelight, maybe even a little champagne. But I guess the sentiment holds up regardless of our surroundings. Rose, I want to marry you.''

Her heart bucked against her ribs. And she felt those roots stretch down again, more firmly this time. Digging in and digging deep. Still, she needed to make some things clear.

"I want a partner, Mason, not a protector or a rescuer. I'm not fragile, you know."

"I know. But maybe being rescued isn't so bad. You rescued me. You came into my life and you reminded me what love was really all about. It's give and take. It can't be one-sided if it's going to last. Ours isn't one-sided."

She nodded, knowing it was true.

"Whatever you want, Rose, I'll give it to you. Just ask."

"I want a family," she said. "I want to belong somewhere, to someone. And I want that someone to be you, that somewhere to be Chance Harbor."

"Is that a yes?" Marnie called out before Mason had a chance to open his mouth.

"Under one condition," she replied and heard the guys from the county groan on Mason's behalf.

"What's the condition?" Marnie asked.

"Hey, do you mind," Mason hollered. "This is my proposal." Glancing back at Rose, he asked, "So, what's the condition?"

"'Highway to Hell' is not going to be our wedding song."

Mason was smiling when he stood, and so was she when he kissed her to a chorus of hoots and hollers.

Even Bergen's Archie Bunkeresque "Oh, jeez," sounded like music to her ears.

"Marriage is all about compromise," Mason said as a misty-eyed Marnie poured a round of celebratory drinks. "What about Van Halen's 'Runnin' with the Devil'?"

"No."

"Um, 'When It's Love'?"

She pulled him close, close enough to feel his heart beat against hers.

"I'll think about it," she promised.

EPILOGUE

THEY settled on Van Halen's "Can't Stop Lovin' You." And spent their honeymoon looking for an apartment in Lansing for Representative-elect Mason Striker.

He'd won the race handily, despite his opponent's mention of Rose's unsavory origins. But, her past hadn't mattered. Not to Mason, nor to the voters who elected him, nor to the town that had adopted her as one of its own. And it no longer mattered to Rose, either.

She still had questions for her biological mother. And, maybe someday, when they were older, she would try to meet her half-sisters. But for now, Marnie was all the sister Rose needed.

Or could handle.

Marnie had taken over the planning of Rose and Mason's wedding, insisting they wait until after her baby was born to marry. She was going to be the matron of honor after all, she'd informed them, and she wanted to look her best in the off-the-shoulder dress she'd picked out. Marnie had even managed to badger Bergen into wearing a tuxedo and walking Rose down the aisle.

Of course, Bergen told Rose he was happy to "give her away." But he'd pecked her cheek before relinquishing her hand to Mason's and then had surprised them both when he'd said in his gravelly voice, "You better be good to her or you'll answer to me."

And Mason had been good to her. Very, very good to her. Just as he'd been very good to the constituents in his state House district for two terms.

Now, as he campaigned for the U.S. Senate, hoping to unseat the very entrenched Bertrand, Rose stood just off stage and listened to him give a speech at a United Auto Workers hall in Flint. She thought about the past several years. They'd been mighty productive ones in so many ways.

Soon, very soon, she thought as she patted her distended abdomen, her husband would have another constituent in his district. Mason, of course, was ecstatic. And perhaps it had been the prospect of becoming a father that had pushed him so hard these past several months. Now his labor had borne fruit. Mason's package of bills to revamp the state foster care system had passed with bipartisan support. The bills would be implemented into law soon.

Rose's Law, Mason had dubbed it.

And Rose knew that even by another name, the changes would be welcomed by the state's silent and largely invisible inhabitants. But the fact that the changes carried *her* name, well, to twist Shakespeare's words—and oh how she now loved to read the Bard—made them twice as sweet.

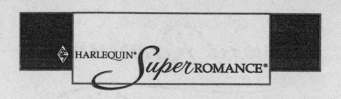
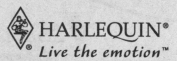

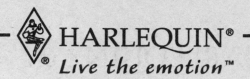

SILHOUETTE Romance

From first love to forever, these love stories
are fairy tale romances for today's woman.

Silhouette Desire

Modern, passionate reads that are powerful and provocative.

Silhouette SPECIAL EDITION™

Emotional, compelling stories that capture the intensity
of living, loving and creating a family in today's world.

Silhouette INTIMATE MOMENTS™

A roller-coaster read that delivers romantic thrills
in a world of suspense, adventure and more.

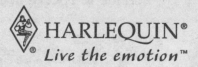

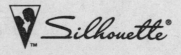